Praise for the novels of

"Allain's writing is wry and delightful."

—*Entertainment Weekly*

"Suzanne Allain delivers a fresh and spirited take on the classic Regency romp. *Mr. Malcolm's List* is a delightful tale that perfectly illustrates the enduring appeal of the Regency romance. It's all here—the fast, witty banter; the elegant ballrooms; the quirky characters; the charming, strong-willed heroine; and the dashing hero who has a thing or two to learn about love."

—*New York Times* bestselling author Amanda Quick

"A merry romp! *Mr. Malcolm's List* is packed with action as one tangled romantic misunderstanding follows fast upon another's heels—to hilarious effect."

—*New York Times* bestselling author Mary Balogh

"Suzanne Allain is a fresh new voice in historical romance. *Mr. Malcolm's List* is a charming, lighthearted confection, with humor, sparkling banter, and gently simmering romantic tension; in other words, classic Regency romance."

—National bestselling author Anne Gracie

"Allain's characters are witty and appealing, and the sizzle between Jeremy and Selina is convincing. This effervescent love story is a charmer." 　　　—*Publishers Weekly*

"Get ready to read well past bedtime with Allain's classic Regency romance and its shrewd, funny heroine, who turns her talent for matchmaking into a match of her own."
—*Library Journal* (starred review)

"Hilarious and fast-paced, *Mr. Malcolm's List* is a bright and refreshing Regency romp." —Shelf Awareness

"Allain adds warmth and the power of female friendships to the appeal of Jane Austen's courtships for a charming Regency romance . . . A delectable escape."
—Historical Novel Society

"A cheeky look at the different expectations placed on men versus women during the Regency era, revealing the limitations society accords individuals in terms of their family connections and personal wealth and education. Both general fiction readers and romance fans looking for a story that will transport them to another time and place, seeking new fictional friends, or hoping to watch characters grow more self-aware and compassionate will revel in this smart love story." —*Booklist* (starred review)

"*Miss Lattimore's Letter* is an entertaining romp through historical London, with plenty of romance, humor, and banter that make this a worthwhile read." —Romance Junkies

"This book is sheer perfection. An adorable, hysterical comedy of manners." —The Romance Dish

"It was witty, hilarious, and contained a cast of upbeat, brooding, and feisty characters that all graced the page with subtle [*Pride and Prejudice*] undertones. I loved it!"

—The Nerd Daily

TITLES BY SUZANNE ALLAIN

Mr. Malcolm's List
Miss Lattimore's Letter
The Ladies Rewrite the Rules
The Wrong Lady Meets Lord Right

The
Wrong Lady
Meets
Lord Right

SUZANNE ALLAIN

BERKLEY ROMANCE

New York

BERKLEY ROMANCE
Published by Berkley
An imprint of Penguin Random House LLC
penguinrandomhouse.com

Copyright © 2024 by Suzanne Allain

BERKLEY and the BERKLEY & B colophon are registered trademarks of
Penguin Random House LLC.

Library of Congress Cataloging-in-Publication Data

Names: Allain, Suzanne, author.
Title: The wrong lady meets lord right / Suzanne Allain.
Description: First Edition. | New York: Berkley Romance, 2024.
Identifiers: LCCN 2024015803 (print) | LCCN 2024015804 (ebook) |
ISBN 9780593549667 (trade paperback) | ISBN 9780593549674 (epub)
Subjects: LCGFT: Romance fiction. | Novels.
Classification: LCC PS3601.L398 W76 2024 (print) |
LCC PS3601.L398 (ebook) |
DDC 813/.6—dc23/eng/20240408
LC record available at https://lccn.loc.gov/2024015803
LC ebook record available at https://lccn.loc.gov/2024015804

First Edition: December 2024

Printed in the United States of America
1st Printing

For all the bookworms

1

Lady Strickland considered it exceedingly vulgar for a lady to display any glimpse of her nether limbs in public, or even to make mention of them. So when she suffered a sudden fit and collapsed, she would have been quite pleased (had she been conscious) that her maid ensured she was decently covered before calling for help. When the doctor finally arrived, Lady Strickland had been dead for a good two hours at least. However, those who knew her felt that her features, hardened by death, differed very little from her usual rigid expression while alive, and had great difficulty believing that she was as dead as the proverbial doornail.

Lady Isabelle, who had been gently informed by her cousin Arabella that her mother had had a sudden apoplexy and there was nothing that could have been done to save her, blinked and nodded, before saying: "Is she asking for me? Should I go to her?"

Bella tried again to explain, stating bluntly: "Issie, your mother is dead." And then, feeling that perhaps she'd been *too* blunt, attempted to soften her pronouncement by saying: "She has gone to her eternal reward."

She felt quite foolish spouting this platitude, as Bella didn't feel her aunt deserved *any* reward, and since God was said to be omniscient, he had to have known it, as well. But Bella was accustomed to protecting her younger cousin from life's harsh realities, and one didn't have to be a high stickler like Lady Strickland had been to realize it was inappropriate to dance a jig on the occasion of your relation's death, no matter how awfully she might have treated you.

Although Bella had no desire to celebrate. Her aunt's passing seemed such an impossible thing to comprehend that she was having difficulty assimilating it and felt no more than a shocked numbness. She could understand Issie's instinctive refusal to accept that her domineering mother, who had tyrannized Issie for the first eighteen years of her life, had ceased to exist.

It became easier to accept in the coming weeks, after the will had been read and Issie had been named the sole beneficiary of the family estate. Bella had no expectation that her aunt would leave her anything so was not surprised when she was proven correct, though she couldn't help feeling a trifle disappointed. However, she was not totally penniless. Her father, who had been the late Lord Strickland's younger brother, had left her a small bequest when he died. (Although her annual income was less than what the Strickland estate spent on candles each year.)

Bella did derive one financial benefit from Lady Strickland's death: while she was alive her aunt had appropriated Bella's income, claiming it was her due for housing and feeding Bella, which she'd done for more than sixteen years since Bella had come to live with the family when she was three years old. Now that Lady Strickland had died, the family's man of affairs was forwarding Bella's allowance directly to her. So even though Bella did not inherit one penny from her miserly aunt, she suddenly felt very wealthy indeed, as she had pocket money for the first time in her life. Unfortunately, she had no opportunity to spend it, as she and Issie never left the estate.

The girls had been surprised to find that, other than that initial visit from the family attorney, they had been left completely to their own devices. Bella finally concluded that Lady Strickland had never expected to die before Issie was married and so had made no arrangements for that eventuality. After all, before Lady Strickland's sudden death, she and Issie had been actively preparing for Issie's come-out and had been planning to travel to London the following week. Therefore Issie and Bella, just eighteen and nineteen, had no older woman to chaperone them. Nor did they have any desire to point out this oversight. They were much happier to be allowed to make their own decisions without criticism, and rejoiced in their freedom from the myriad rules and restrictions Lady Strickland had imposed on them. This freedom was limited, however, as they were expected to observe strict mourning, and Bella couldn't help feeling that even though Lady Strickland was gone, the conventions that she had insisted upon were continuing to control them.

But a year couldn't last forever, and eleven months after her aunt's death, Bella approached Issie in order to discuss their future. She had no doubts about where she would find her cousin, and when she entered the library—a much cozier room compared to when her aunt was alive—she found Issie curled up on a sofa reading by the light of a candle, exactly where Bella expected her to be.

It was only midmorning but it was a cold, damp, cloudy day in late February, and one indulgence they'd granted themselves since Lady Strickland's passing was the lighting of fires and candles in any room they pleased. And Issie's favorite room was the library. Bella enjoyed reading, too, but not nearly as much as Issie, who had to be reminded to eat and sleep when she was engrossed in a book.

Issie didn't look up when Bella entered the room and, even after Bella cleared her throat, Issie merely gave her an absentminded smile and a nod before retreating once again into her book.

"Issie," Bella said.

"Yes?" she replied, though she wasn't looking at Bella when she did so.

"Issie, give it to me."

This finally got Issie's attention. She pulled the book tight against her chest as if she were its mother and it was an infant that Bella was trying to forcibly wrest from her arms. "Why?"

"I need to talk to you, and I need you to pay attention."

Issie sighed, but obediently handed the book to Bella, though she looked bereft as she did so. Bella, looking more closely at her cousin, was surprised by her unhealthy appearance. As critical and dictatorial as Lady Strickland had been, she was better than Bella at making sure Issie ate, slept, and left the house. In the eleven months since her mother had died, Issie had become a virtual hermit. She hardly ever dressed for dinner, and she and Bella very rarely ate in the dining room, contenting themselves with a tray in their rooms. They never went to church or into the village, or paid or received calls, and Bella at first had been happy about this state of affairs, as she felt that if she and Issie were seen in public without an older female chaperone, one of their officious neighbors might take it upon themselves to contact someone who had the authority to appoint one. But now she felt guilty that she had let her cousin deteriorate to this point, and wondered if having an older female companion would have been such a bad thing, after all. It was highly unlikely that anyone could be as harsh a taskmaster as Lady Strickland.

And Bella acknowledged that, while Lady Strickland had been far *too* demanding of Issie, Bella had not been demanding enough. Bella knew, more than anyone, how her cousin had suffered under her mother's merciless domination, and so was inclined to give in to Issie too easily, condoning behavior that could not be for her long-term good.

Why, Issie had dark circles around her eyes, was white as a sheet, and seemed even thinner than she had been before Lady Strickland's death, and she had been slender then.

Bella felt a sudden surge of sympathy for her poor, rich cousin, and asked very kindly: "Dearest Issie, isn't there anything you would like to do?"

"What do you mean?" Issie asked.

"Our year of mourning will end in a few weeks. Wouldn't you like to go to London? You were on the verge of going when your mother died. Just think, in less than a month it will be permissible for you to attend balls, and musical concerts, and the theatre . . . oh! I envy you prodigiously!" Bella said, in all sincerity. She knew her common birth and lack of fortune made it impossible for her to have her own come-out, and gave herself frequent lectures so that she did not feel depressed or discontented when comparing her circumstances with her cousin's.

However, rather than being pleased at this list of delights that awaited her, Issie appeared horrified. She put one hand to her heart and her breathing accelerated, as if the very thought of such activities caused her extreme agitation. "I do not want to do *any* of those things! I know you mean well, Bella, but please do not worry about me. I am quite content. Indeed, I am doing everything I've ever desired to do."

"But . . . you don't do anything; other than stay indoors and read."

"Exactly!" her cousin replied, and a brilliant smile lit her pale face.

Bella did her best to convince Issie to join her in rides and walks, but Issie pleaded poor health and staunchly refused every invitation. Bella was wondering if she should approach someone older and wiser for advice, and even paid a visit to the vicarage, her first time making a call since her aunt's death. However, while the vicar and his wife were at least two decades older than Bella, they didn't strike her as particularly wiser, and she decided against confiding her troubles in them.

Before she could worry for too much longer, a letter arrived for Isabelle that Bella felt was the answer to their dilemma. However, Issie eyed it as if it were a snake, particularly when she saw who it was from. "Who is Lady Dutton?" Bella asked, looking over Issie's shoulder.

"Mama's aunt. My great-aunt," Issie replied.

"Have you ever met her?" Bella did not recall meeting her, but she had never left Fenborough Hall since she'd arrived there as a child; whereas Issie had gone with her mother to visit relatives upon occasion.

"Once; on a visit to London when I was twelve. She told my mother if she allowed me to read so much I would ruin my eyesight and spoil my looks and no man would marry me. Mama forbade me to read for the entire month of our visit." Issie looked as if the injustice of this incident still rankled seven years later. Then her indignant expression turned mischievous. "But I snuck a book and candle into bed every night. One time I nearly caught the bed hangings on fire, and I slept till noon every day, but I was never found out."

Issie was smiling fondly over this memory when she began reading the letter, but her smile quickly faded. "Oh, no, it's the worst possible news!"

Issie handed Bella the letter and sank down onto the sofa. She looked even paler than she had before, something Bella had not thought possible.

"Issie, are you all right? Should I get your vinaigrette?" Bella asked.

"Just read the letter," Issie whispered, and Bella took a deep breath to prepare herself for whatever dire news it contained. She couldn't imagine what could have caused Issie's stricken expression. They had already lost their closest relatives, so no one could have died, or at least no one Issie cared about. Had Issie's fortune been lost? Had Napoleon escaped a second time? Had Lady Strickland faked her death, and was she about to reappear now that their year of mourning was ending?

Bella's own knees got a little weak at that last thought, and she dropped down next to Issie on the sofa. But even though she read the letter twice, once very quickly and a second time much more thoroughly in case she'd missed something, she couldn't find anything that would have caused Issie's dismayed reaction. In fact, Bella thought it was the most thrilling letter she'd ever read, even though Lady Dutton had atrocious spelling, grammar, and penmanship. Perhaps *that* was what had upset Issie so.

Bella looked up from the letter to see Issie watching her

with an expression of concern. "Issie, we're going to London!" Bella shouted jubilantly, jumping up from the sofa and twirling around the room before running back to her cousin's side and hugging her.

Issie groaned.

It was apparent that Lady Dutton assumed Issie's governess was still in residence, as her letter suggested that the girls travel to London under her escort. They were to stay at Lady Dutton's London house for the season, and she intended to give Isabelle the come-out she'd missed because of her mother's demise. (Though she'd spelled it "dumyes" and it had taken Bella a good ten seconds to figure out that Lady Dutton wasn't offering Lady Strickland an insult.) Lady Dutton had specifically included Bella in the invitation. At least, that's how Bella interpreted the paragraph that said if Issie's cousin was still living with her she might as well bring her and they'd find something for her to do, since Lady Dutton was honor bound to show the same charity toward the "poor, unforchunet creacher" that Lady Strickland had.

If it were up to Issie, she would have found some way of ignoring the summons. She'd even suggested to Bella that they destroy the letter and pretend it had been lost, but Bella responded very reasonably that Lady Dutton would then send someone to get them or come herself, and that would only have the effect of delaying the inevitable and make Lady Dutton annoyed with them. By repeatedly reminding Issie of such facts, Bella was eventually able to coax her into a carriage and onto the road to London.

Bella was highly impressed with herself for accomplishing this feat, and reflected that it was a shame there was no one to notice and praise her as she deserved. Issie sulked in the corner of the carriage, and May, the fifteen-year-old maidservant they'd brought with them, was just as bashful and nervous as her mistress. Bella assumed that was why Issie had chosen her to accompany them, so that Bella would have no one to support her in what Issie insisted on calling "this mad and ridiculous escapade."

It *was* somewhat mad, Bella admitted to herself, as while Issie had traveled with her mother occasionally, Bella had never been any further than a few miles from Fenborough Hall. She couldn't believe that she was twenty years old and only now leaving. She knew less about travel than Issie did, perhaps even less than May, who had a cousin in "London-town."

However, with the help of their coachman, who had made a few trips to London while Lady Strickland was alive, combined with Bella's fierce determination to begin this new chapter in her life as soon as possible, Bella and Issie made it safely to London.

Upon their arrival, the young women were ushered into an opulent drawing room where Lady Dutton was waiting to greet them. Bella was sorry that they were not even allowed the opportunity to refresh themselves before meeting her and hoped the interview wouldn't be a long one. But since Lady Dutton stood at their entrance and didn't invite them to sit, it appeared as if their ordeal was to be brief.

Lady Dutton's critical glance quickly passed over the three young women before settling on the diminutive May.

"Who is this? She's certainly not your governess; she looks to be no more than a child. Who are you, girl?" Lady Dutton asked her.

"May-your-ladyship." May was so overcome with fear at addressing this august personage that the sentence came out in a hurried, breathy whisper.

Lady Dutton did not deign to reply, but merely looked down her nose at the lowly chambermaid in a silence that dragged on for an excruciatingly long time, until poor little May was visibly shaking. Then, finally, Lady Dutton asked: "May I what?"

To which question May was incapable of responding, merely staring at Lady Dutton in confused terror while her mouth opened and closed several times.

Lady Dutton turned in exasperation to Bella, whom she'd obviously marked as the only conversable member of the group, and asked: "What is wrong with the girl? Why can't she finish her sentence?"

"She had finished. She was telling you her name. It's 'May,' my lady," Bella explained.

"Call me Aunt Lucretia, child," Lady Dutton replied, and a wave of relief washed over Bella. She'd never expected a relation of Lady Strickland's to treat her so graciously and had prepared herself to face coldness, if not outright insults, so she was very pleased to be proven wrong in her assumptions.

Now that Lady Dutton realized that the maid had merely been giving her name, she quickly, albeit firmly, dismissed the girl, telling her that she could stay for two days but was then to return with the coachman to Oxfordshire. Bella was relieved that the question of the missing governess appeared to have been forgotten. After May had gratefully left the room, still trembling from her encounter with Lady Dutton, that lady turned to survey the cousins, who moved closer to each other in an unconscious seeking of support.

"Why, you're as alike as two peas in a pod," she finally said, before the silence had grown too ominous. "How does anyone tell you apart?"

Bella and Issie looked at each other in surprise. There was a superficial resemblance, to be sure. They both had blue eyes and brown hair, but while Issie's was a mousy brown, Bella's was a darker, richer chestnut. And while they were of a similar height, a little taller than average, Issie was thinner and smaller-bosomed. Both girls were attractive, but Issie's conventional prettiness paled in comparison to Bella's more striking appearance, as Bella's features were more defined; her lips fuller, her blue eyes a more vibrant hue, and her complexion blooming with health. Only a woman who was nearsighted and too vain to wear spectacles would ever think the two girls could pass for each other.

But they had no desire to argue with the lady and allowed her statement to go unchallenged, and she continued: "Though I'm sure *I* will have no problem knowing who is who, as Isabelle is my dear niece's daughter, and blood is thicker than water, as the saying goes." She seemed ready to bring the interview to an end, and gestured to the door, where the housekeeper had suddenly appeared. "You would probably like to refresh yourselves after your long journey. Mrs. Lucas will show you to your rooms." Before they could leave, she turned to address Issie directly. "You are called Arabella, are you not?" she asked, and the two girls stared back at her as witlessly as May had.

Bella, realizing that the lady had confused her and Issie for each other, hurried to correct her. "Aunt Lucretia," she said, before pausing, as it had suddenly occurred to her that she'd been invited to call her that because the lady thought she was Isabelle. Should she address her by her title after all? Then she thought about how awkward it would be to correct Lady Dutton when she'd just announced that the noble blood she and Issie shared would create a special bond between them.

While Bella hesitated, Issie startled her by saying, very clearly: "Yes, I am called Arabella."

Bella waited until they were shown to their respective guest rooms, the *wrong* guest rooms, and after Mrs. Lucas had left Bella alone, she immediately went into the room Issie now inhabited to confront her. "Why did you tell your great-aunt that you were Arabella? That you were me? I.

That you were I?" She paused to listen to herself. It sounded awkward no matter how she phrased it. "Oh, you know what I mean."

"It didn't seem very tactful to correct her at that moment," Issie responded reasonably. "We can just tell her the next time we're together; she'll never know the difference. She's obviously nearsighted, poor thing."

"That's true," Bella replied, though she wondered if Issie was telling the *entire* truth. She couldn't help but feel Issie was up to something. Her cousin wasn't a devious person, but because she'd been oppressed by her mother for so long, she'd become skilled at quietly and unobtrusively getting her own way on the rare occasions that she could. However, Bella couldn't imagine how it would benefit Issie to assume Bella's identity as the poor, unloved, unwanted daughter of a misalliance. Even this brief masquerade had demonstrated the inequality of their treatment, as Bella pointed out to Issie. "But you've been given the wrong room. I'm sure the grand chamber I was assigned was really intended for you."

"I prefer this one. It's cozy," Issie said.

Bella looked around her. It wasn't a *bad* room; she doubted there was a bad room in the house, unless it was in the servants' quarters. But it was simpler and smaller than the room Bella had just been assigned, when she was presumed to be "Lady Isabelle." The four-poster bed in that room had rose velvet draperies, and the walls were covered with a lovely light green Chinese-style paper painted with peacocks and flowering trees. Bella had felt an actual pang at the realization she'd have to give up the room after they'd corrected the misunderstanding concerning their identities. But for some reason Issie didn't want the beautifully decorated room. Perhaps she planned to read in bed and didn't want to get caught by her great-aunt.

"Are you afraid Aunt Lucretia will take your books away? Or that you'll catch the bed hangings on fire?" Bella asked.

Issie shrugged. "That's definitely a consideration. Though mostly it's because I don't like a lot of attention from the servants. And I thought it would make a nice change if *you* received special treatment, for once."

Bella smiled fondly at her cousin. "That's very kind of you, Issie. Thank you."

Issie nodded and pulled a book out of her reticule. And Bella, realizing that their conversation was at an end, returned to her own luxurious chamber.

Over the coming days, Bella and Issie found that Lady Dutton frequently confused them for each other, and they dealt with it by pretending to be whomever it was she mistook them for. This seemed easier than embarrassing her by constantly correcting her.

However, when Lord Dutton made an appearance, they worried that they might have to change their tactics. He was not nearsighted (in fact, he appeared to see far too much), and he would catch on to their little ploy immediately.

It was the second morning of their stay before Bella even

realized he was in residence. She came down for breakfast to find an elderly gentleman seated at the table reading a newspaper.

Bella had walked a few feet into the room before noticing his presence, and when she did, she came to a sudden stop. "Oh! I beg your pardon," she said.

He looked regretfully at his paper for a moment before rising unhurriedly to his feet and bowing slightly in her direction. He was a very dapper, elegant gentleman of around seventy, with impeccably coiffed gray hair. To Bella he appeared the very epitome of an aristocrat.

"Good morning," he said. "You must be Lady Isabelle."

Bella hesitated a moment before deciding she should be truthful. "No, I'm Isabelle's cousin, Arabella Grant."

"Miss Grant." He gestured to the sideboard. "Please."

Bella hurriedly filled a plate, hardly knowing what she chose, as she hated for him to stand there waiting while his coffee grew cold, and he was obviously too much the gentleman to sit until after she had.

Her plate full, she rushed to the table and sat down, and he proceeded to do so as well, eyeing his newspaper with a look of longing.

"Please, my lord, do not stand upon ceremony with me. You're more than welcome to read." Bella would actually prefer for him to read his paper, as she felt exceedingly uncomfortable eating in front of him, certain he'd find something to criticize in the way that she did so

His lips turned up so slightly that Bella barely recognized it as a smile, before he did as she'd suggested and picked up his paper.

Bella was very uncomfortable eating breakfast with this formidable, silent gentleman and regretted that she'd come down. She should have done as Issie had and requested a tray in her chamber, but before she could make her escape, Lady Dutton entered the room.

"My lord," she greeted her husband.

He answered her with a slight inclination of his head.

"And Isabelle," she continued, nodding her head in Bella's direction.

Bella looked at Lord Dutton, a stricken expression on her face, unsure how to answer since she'd just told him she *wasn't* Isabelle. But before she could respond, Lord Dutton had risen from his seat and was speaking.

"Enjoy your breakfast. I'm off to my club," he said, and left the room.

Bella *was* able to enjoy her breakfast after the intimidating nobleman had left, though as Lady Dutton had confused her with Issie, she was forced to listen to instructions about the court presentation she wouldn't be participating in. She cheerfully responded, "Yes, Aunt Lucretia," whenever necessary and had a second cup of tea.

2

Have you gone mad, Issie?" Bella asked, and immediately regretted her harsh words when she saw Issie wince in response. However, Bella did feel her remark was justified, as Issie had just told her she was far too ill to go to court and had begged Bella to take her place and assume her identity, while being presented to Her Royal Highness, the *Queen of England*!

"I know it's a lot to ask of you, but I just cannot do it!" Issie said.

Looking at her as she lay in bed, Bella had to admit that Issie appeared very ill indeed. She didn't have the strength to rise and was trembling uncontrollably.

"What exactly is wrong?" Bella asked, in a much kinder tone. "Should I send for a doctor?"

"No, please don't. I don't want to see anyone. I'm very weak, and I'm having palpitations," Issie said, clutching her chest. "I have this awful feeling that if I kneel in front of the queen I'll drop dead like my mother did."

"At least your legs would be covered," Bella said, as the court dress had the most ridiculously long train she'd ever seen. But then she chided herself for making inappropriate jokes when Issie was in such a sad state. "I'm sorry, but I just don't see how it's possible. We should tell Aunt Lucretia that you're ill and ask if your presentation can be postponed."

"No! I can't postpone it. I'll feel even worse if I have to live in dread of doing it again at a later date. I just need it to be over and done with."

Bella continued to argue against the idea, but seeing that her cousin was sincerely agitated and she was looking weaker the longer Bella refused, Bella finally capitulated to Issie's request.

"Thank you, Bella. I'll never forget this," Issie said faintly, before sinking further down into the pillows and closing her eyes.

Bella told herself that Issie had better not forget it, because it was the most selfless, terrifying thing she'd ever agreed to do. Only daughters or wives of peers were invited to make their presentation at court, and if it was discovered that she was there impersonating her noble cousin, Bella couldn't even imagine what the consequences might be. Also, she'd seen Issie's presentation gown, and it was an unwieldy monstrosity. Bella wouldn't be surprised if the thought of having to wear it was what had sickened Issie.

The presentation was that very day, but Bella still had four or five hours before she had to leave the house, as Issie had sent a maid to Bella's room to awaken her before dawn. Bella reflected that, although she had initially been annoyed at being awoken so early from a sound sleep, it was a very good thing she had been as she would need every spare minute to get into the dress and its many accoutrements.

There were very stringent rules about court dress, and Queen Charlotte's guests were required to wear the hooped skirts that were the custom in her youth. But as the waist had been allowed to rise in deference to current fashions, the dresses were oddly bell-shaped, the bodice looking disproportionately small in comparison with the ballooning skirt with its long train. Bella wondered if it was in an attempt to offset this strange silhouette that the headdresses were so very large, as one of the other strict codes of court attire was that every lady was required to wear feathers in her hair.

As she was being helped into her hoops and dress, Bella wondered what the servants thought of her and Issie's odd behavior. It was Bella who had been presented to them as Lady Isabelle that first day, but it was Issie who had been fitted for the dress, and now Bella was the one wearing it. And the ramifications of this were soon plain to see, as the bodice, which had been tailored for Lady Isabelle's slighter figure, looked positively indecent on Bella.

"I'll take the dress off, and we can sew some lace on," Bella suggested, and Nancy, the maid who had been helping Bella dress, looked at her as if she'd taken leave of her senses.

"Beg pardon, miss, um, milady," Nancy said hesitantly, obviously unsure how she should address Bella, before giving up on any form of address and continuing her protest. "It took us a good half hour to get you into it. We don't have time to be starting all over again."

"Then sew the lace on while I'm wearing it," Bella suggested. Nancy was hesitant to do this as well, as the bodice was so very tight it would be easy to prick Bella with the needle in a *very* sensitive location. But finally, after Bella insisted, Nancy put in one or two stitches while stuffing the lace down the front of the dress as best she could, and Bella reflected on the fact that Nancy might not know her true identity, but she was now extremely familiar with her anatomy.

Nancy went to retrieve Issie's jewels, returning a few minutes later with a box that contained a diamond necklace and diamond chandelier eardrops. Bella had mixed feelings when the maidservant clasped the jewelry around her neck. On the one hand, she was relieved she was going to have *something* to cover the vast amount of exposed bosom (as the lace had helped very little), while on the other hand, she was extremely anxious over the thought of wearing a fortune in jewels that did not belong to her.

But it was now time to meet Aunt Lucretia, and Bella found her attention fully occupied with trying to accomplish something she thought she'd mastered when she was two years old. walking. Nancy was at her side to help carry her train, but between the hoops and the feathers, Bella had a very difficult time negotiating the stairs. She couldn't see her feet at all, something she'd never before realized was a necessary part of the walking process. She found herself descending crab-like, holding very tightly to the railing with both hands and stepping sideways one tentative foot at a time.

Aunt Lucretia had been waiting in the drawing room and did not emerge into the front hall until Bella was at the very end of her performance, so Bella was greeted with smiles and compliments instead of exhortations to hurry.

"You look stunning, my dear," said the woman who couldn't see her. "Absolutely stunning."

Bella realized she probably did look good to someone who was nearsighted and saw her as a great blur of white and pale pink satin, sparkling diamonds, and fluffy, waving feathers. So she thanked Aunt Lucretia and smiled at her, though her smile quickly faded when the butler opened the front door and she realized she now had to maneuver herself into a carriage.

Bella wasn't very impressed with St. James's Palace, but it could have been because the exterior, with its dark brick facade and imposing turrets, reminded Bella of a prison and she already felt like a criminal, impersonating her cousin as she was. King Henry VIII had built the palace for Anne Boleyn, and their intertwining initials were still to be found inscribed above at least one of the many fireplaces. Thinking of the former queen's disastrous end made Bella wonder if the universe was trying to warn her about what happens to scheming young women who bring themselves to the attention of royalty.

The interior of St. James's Palace was far grander, and Bella preferred it over the exterior; especially the queen's drawing room with its crimson velvet window hangings, high ceilings, and tapestry-covered walls. At first, she found it odd that the room was almost empty of furniture, but then she remembered that no one was allowed to sit in the presence of the queen. And perhaps it was just as well, because Bella had had enough difficulties seating herself in the carriage.

After they entered the room, Aunt Lucretia exchanged greetings with some of the ladies present before introducing Bella to them. Bella hid her face behind her fan and said as little as possible during these introductions, and then thought about what a poor impression she was making as "Lady Isabelle." Still, it was better that London society think Issie was awkward and shy than accuse her of being someone else entirely when she finally began going out. And Issie *was* somewhat awkward and shy.

However, the longer Bella had to wait for her presentation, the more nervous she became. She suddenly remembered that Aunt Lucretia had told her (during the lecture she'd scarcely listened to) that she was to back away from the queen after she curtsied, as it was not permissible to turn one's back on royalty. Bella began to think she had to have some practice, as she had difficulties walking at all in her present costume, and couldn't even imagine attempting to walk *backward*.

Bella was able to slip away from Aunt Lucretia's side,

first into a hall and finally into an antechamber that was empty. Or so she thought. But the annoying headdress with its feathers and dangling lappets must have interfered with her peripheral vision because, when turning to look behind her to make sure no one had seen her leave, she collided quite forcefully with a gentleman.

She found herself plastered to his chest with his arms around her, as he had instinctively clasped her to him in order to prevent her from falling. She was very grateful for this, as she had struck him so hard that she felt a little out of breath and unsteady on her feet.

But her dizziness only worsened when she finally raised her head and saw his face.

"I beg your pardon," Bella said, blinking up at the gentleman. She had a dazed impression of warm brown eyes in a tanned face looking intently into her own, but her senses were overwhelmed by the feel of his firm chest pressed against hers and his hands on her bare arms above her gloves, so that she was unable to make a rational judgment about his appearance. Her irrational judgment was that he was devastatingly attractive, and she had no desire to step away from him in order to view him from a distance and form a more objective opinion.

Lord Brooke, who had been leaving St. James's Palace when this woman appeared from nowhere and hurled herself into his arms, did the gentlemanly thing and claimed responsibility for the mishap.

"It was my fault entirely," he said, even though he was still unsure how he'd come to be holding a frilly and fluffy, not to mention sweetly scented and rounded, young woman.

"Oh, I don't know," the lady replied with a smile. "I think these feathers must share some of the blame, don't you?"

Lord Brooke returned her smile, even though the thought that he must now release her was starting to cause him a degree of regret. As he reluctantly stepped away, he was struck by a chilling draft. His chest, even though well covered by a waistcoat and jacket, felt bereft without her bosom pressed against it. Still smiling, however, he agreed with her that the feathers were gravely at fault.

"I've never even seen an actual ostrich, have you?" she asked him. "Yet there must be enough feathers in the queen's drawing room to coat a dozen of them, as well as a few egrets. I had never before considered it, but it must hurt when they're plucked, poor things." Her eyes grew wide as an even more horrific thought occurred to her. "You don't think they kill—"

He hurried to interrupt before he was forced to answer that particular question. "I assume you're here to be presented to the queen?" She nodded in response, her feathers bobbing. "Then you should probably return to the drawing room, you know. It would cause a minor scandal if you weren't there when your name was called."

"Would it? I see," the young lady said. "Then I suppose I have no choice but to return."

She looked up at him with a wistful smile, and he wished he could tell her that she did not have to return after all, that she could run away immediately, with him, preferably. He wasn't sure what her specific fear was, but hoping to dispel it, said, "There's no need to worry. It happens very quickly, once they call for you. The queen might ask how your family does and send her regards to one of your relations, but it will all be over before you know it."

"As long as I don't trip over my skirt while backing away. I'm not very skilled at maneuvering in *this*." She made a graceful wave of her hand, gesturing from her chin to her feet to demonstrate what she was talking about, so that Lord Brooke allowed his gaze to follow where he had been keeping himself from looking. Court dress was somewhat ludicrous in his view, with its overly festooned hoop skirts and feathered headdresses and lappets, but the diamonds she was wearing around her regal neck were crowning one of the most splendid sets of bosoms he'd ever seen.

Lord Brooke rather desperately returned his gaze to her lovely face, but any relief he felt was to be short-lived. "Would you mind if I practiced my curtsy?" she asked. "I would hate to stumble and fall in front of the queen. And I didn't have the opportunity to practice as much as I should have."

Taking his silence as agreement, she suddenly swept down in front of him. "Well?" she asked, peeping up at him through one of her feathers.

"Bravo," he said, and put out a hand to help her rise, while nobly averting his gaze.

"That's very kind of you, but you shouldn't help me. I must practice the most difficult part: my exit," she said, and she backed away from him slowly, biting down slightly on her full bottom lip in an expression of intense concentration, which caused Lord Brooke to focus *his* concentration on her mouth. This did not do anything to elevate his thoughts, though at least the temperature seemed to be rising, and he no longer felt the least bit chilled.

The lady had successfully backed a good ten feet away from him before she stopped, looking at him with one slightly raised eyebrow.

"That was excellent. Very graceful," he commended her, and her face lit up in response.

"I'm sure you're flattering me; I'm probably about as graceful as a pouter pigeon, but thank you," she said. "And now, unfortunately, I must go back."

She gave a little wave of farewell and he held up his hand as well, though he was unsure if he was returning her gesture or asking her not to go. But she was gone as quickly as she'd appeared and he was left standing there with his hand held out.

He spent a moment wondering if he should leave as he'd intended, but decided instead to follow the young lady, his curiosity too great to allow her to disappear without learning her name. He made his way to one of the chambers that overlooked the queen's drawing room and scanned the crowd. He finally caught sight of "his" lady standing beside Lady Dutton. Even though her face was mostly hidden by the fan she held in front of it, there was no mistaking the dress, or that figure. He wondered how it was that she had been able to converse so openly and comfortably with him with no hint of shyness, when she was apparently so un-nerved by her presentation that she had run from the room and was even now hiding behind her fan.

The fact that she was accompanying Lady Dutton should have given him a clue as to her identity, and thus he should not have been as surprised as he was when the Lord Chamberlain announced her name.

"Lady Isabelle Grant."

"Good God," said Lord Brooke, and immediately left the palace.

Lord Brooke had last seen Lady Isabelle more than five years ago, shortly before his mother's death, when Lady Strickland had paid them a visit with her daughter in tow. Isabelle had been thirteen, perhaps fourteen; he could not remember exactly. She had still been a child, however, and he realized that the last stage of growth before adulthood was one of major transformation. Even so, he would never have recognized her as the woman he'd just met. Five or six years ago she'd been a pale ghost of a girl, extremely shy, and had refused to even look at him, staring resolutely at the floor her entire visit. He couldn't remember her saying more than a few words, and those were spoken in a whisper. He was convinced her mother was to blame; Lady Strickland had been so very domineering he had felt that Lady Isabelle would never be allowed to exert her own personality, or even develop one.

Therefore, the vibrant, animated creature he'd collided

with in the halls of St. James's Palace was a shock to him in more ways than one. Now that he knew her identity and he was removed from her actual presence, he was beginning to doubt his impression of her. Could it be that her physical beauty had made her seem more captivating than she actually was? He would not be the first man to be taken in by an attractive facade.

But he hadn't imagined her open, confiding manner; her engaging smile; her sparkling charm. He'd observed none of these characteristics, or even the potential for them, when they'd last met. How had Lady Isabelle developed into such an enchanting creature?

Of course, she hadn't recognized him, either, and he had changed far less than she had, as he had been in his early twenties at their last meeting. So perhaps memory wasn't the most reliable standard for judgment.

Still, he felt there was a definite mystery about the Lady Isabelle. And he was just the man to unravel it.

As soon as Bella returned from the presentation and had changed into a more comfortable gown, she rushed into Issie's room to see if her condition had improved. She was disappointed to find her cousin still in bed.

Issie looked up anxiously at Bella's entrance and asked, "How did it go?" at the same time Bella asked, "How do you feel?"

"Fine," Bella said, while Issie simultaneously answered: "Terrible."

"No one suspected that you were not me?" Issie asked.

"I don't see how anyone could have. Though they probably think you very strange indeed, as I spoke in monosyllables and kept my fan in front of my face the entire time."

"I care naught what they think of me. I doubt I will ever meet any of them."

"What do you mean? Aunt Lucretia said now that I, meaning you, have been presented, she is going to start taking me, I mean you, on morning calls. And apparently there's a musical concert in two nights, and an opera the night after that, and oh! You've been invited to a ball!" Bella said, thinking this information would give Issie something to anticipate and assist her in making a quick recovery.

Issie shuddered and put her hands over her face. "I can't do it, Bella."

"Then we must tell Aunt Lucretia that you're ill and send for a doctor."

"I doubt a doctor will be able to do anything for me. I am definitely not capable of embarking upon a round of *social* activities," Issie said with a distasteful grimace, as if she were being offered some fish that was off.

Bella sat on the bed next to her cousin and took her hands in hers. "Issie, are you sure that you're physically incapable of these things, or is it merely that you don't *want* to do them?"

Issie looked up at Bella, her eyes watery. "I am not lying to you, Bella. It's true that I don't want to participate, but neither am I well enough to do so even if I *did* want to."

Bella looked sympathetically at her sickly cousin. She

herself was very healthy, and it saddened her to see Issie in such a state. Issie finally broke the silence to say, somewhat hesitantly, "Bella, what if . . . you continued to take my place?"

"What? That's a nonsensical idea. I only went today because it was just this once, and I knew how much money had been spent on that ridiculous dress and how disappointed Aunt Lucretia would have been if you'd cancelled. And there is something to be said for getting the whole thing over with, as you mentioned. But I have no intention of masquerading as you for the rest of the season."

"But . . . why couldn't you? Whom would it hurt if you did so? Operas and concerts and balls are all things that *you* would enjoy, and 'Arabella Grant' would never be invited to hobnob with high society. This would be your opportunity to experience things you'd only dreamt of. Just think, too, how pleased Aunt Lucretia would be if she believed she'd given me the come-out she'd promised my mother. She'd be so disappointed if I told her I can't do the season, especially after she's spent a fortune outfitting me in new clothes."

"Yes, Issie, what about those new clothes? We're not exactly the same size, you know. I was mortified to appear in such a tight-fitting dress today."

Issie waved her hand as if this was of little importance. "You're a very good seamstress, Bella. You can alter them to fit or get one of the maids to do so."

"But Issie, you forget why Aunt Lucretia is doing this in the first place: to find *you* a husband. I can't marry someone in your place; I have no intention of posing as you for the rest of my life! And even if I temporarily agreed to it, I would attract so much attention when the extent of your fortune and family connections were known that the gentlemen would rush to court the lady I was presumed to be. What if I received a proposal of marriage? Any man would be rightly incensed to be presented with an entirely different woman at the altar."

A faraway expression appeared on Issie's face, similar to when she was engrossed in a book. "Like Jacob and Rachel," she murmured, and Bella realized her cousin was no longer paying her any attention, that she was lost in her imaginings of a couple she'd read about.

"Yes, but that happened in ancient times. We live in a more advanced age, and no one substitutes one woman for another on her wedding night."

"But Bella, haven't you ever wondered how their father got away with it? Did Jacob not look at Leah's face at all while they were . . . *you* know," Issie said.

"I do *not* know, and neither do you!" Bella said. And then was surprised to find herself laughing. Issie chuckled softly as well, and Bella was relieved her cousin wasn't so ill that she had lost her sense of humor. "At any rate, I think you've made my point. Think of how angry Jacob was when he was tricked into marrying the wrong woman, and all the problems that resulted. I cannot pretend to be you. You must participate in your season so that you can find yourself a husband."

"I don't want a husband!" Issie protested. "If I'm not well

enough to go to a ball, I'm certainly not well enough to get married! I wish you would consider helping me, Bella. We are to stay less than three months, and we are more than halfway through the first one; surely, you could stave off proposals of marriage for a mere two months more. It would solve all our problems, and I could find enjoyment through your enjoyment."

Bella sighed. "I promise to think about it, but only if *you* promise to see a doctor."

"Very well," Issie agreed, with a sigh of her own.

3

A doctor did come to see Issie, and Bella was concerned that the examination would kill her before her mysterious illness could.

When Issie and Bella discussed it later, they very magnanimously agreed that it wasn't *entirely* Dr. Jordan's fault that he had exacerbated Issie's nervous condition. He was not to blame that their only experience of doctors thus far had been with the middle-aged, rotund, balding fellow who was Lady Strickland's physician, and who one could only imagine had emerged from his mother's womb as a nondescript fatherly figure. Certainly, he could never have been a personable man like this one, who was no more than five and twenty years of age, with tousled blond hair that he had not had the time to cut, so that he had to frequently sweep it out of his hazel eyes. Based on their previous experience with members of the medical profession, neither Issie nor

Bella had expected to meet such a handsome young doctor. And Issie was worried about how she could hide her attraction to him while he was inspecting her from head to toe.

Bella thought Issie would have found the doctor's visit excruciatingly awkward and embarrassing, in any event, as no other human had touched either of them as familiarly as Dr. Jordan proceeded to touch Issie during his examination. (Though Nancy had come close to doing so when she'd had her hands down Bella's bodice.)

Merely his visit to her bedchamber, as unthreatening as he tried to be with his calm, polite demeanor and softly voiced questions, overwhelmed poor Issie. She clutched at her chest and began breathing even more shallowly than before, so that Bella could only surmise her palpitations had increased in severity.

The previous evening Issie had insisted on bathing and washing her hair, and this morning Bella had helped her to sit upright in bed, with a pillow behind her back. Issie made a very pretty invalid, as the increased activity, as limited as it was, along with the reflection from her pink morning gown, had put a tinge of color in her pale cheeks, and her brown curls were fluffy from their recent washing. The doctor, after asking what her symptoms included and learning that she had no cough or pain but was experiencing weakness, palpitations, and nervous attacks, told her he needed to listen to her heart, which he did by placing his ear against her chest.

Issie gasped.

"Please breathe normally, Miss . . ." the doctor said, his ear still pressed against her breast.

"Grant," Issie whispered, and Bella realized that Issie was again assuming Bella's identity, though Bella was unsure of her reason. Perhaps Issie did not feel she should take the time to identify herself as "Lady Isabelle" at the same time the doctor was attempting to listen to her heart, or she did not wish to embarrass him by pointing out her exalted rank. Bella did not correct him, either, deciding it scarcely mattered if Dr. Jordan failed to use Issie's title while he had his cheek pressed against her bosom.

"Could you please cough?" he asked a moment later, though to Issie, waiting in silence and acutely aware of every breath she took, it felt like an eternity had passed.

Issie dutifully coughed, and the doctor finally raised his head from her chest, his blond locks even more disordered than before.

"It doesn't sound as if you have any fluid in your lungs," he told Issie, who just stared at him with big eyes. "But your heart rate is quite elevated and your pulse quick and light." He briefly pressed on Issie's lower stomach and she gasped in shock. "I beg your pardon; I had to check for accumulation of fluid in your abdomen." He drew back a little, but looked Issie over so carefully that Bella felt even more sympathy for her, as she would not have wanted to be on the receiving end of such a comprehensive perusal. This doctor was much more thorough than Lady Strickland's physician had ever been. Perhaps that was why Lady Strickland was dead.

But Dr. Jordan wasn't finished and reached for Issie's hands next. "Your hands are too cold," he said, after squeezing each one in turn, "but don't appear to be swollen."

He placed her hands by her sides and reached for the blanket that covered her feet. "I beg your pardon, Miss Grant, but I must examine your . . . other extremities as well," he said, turning slightly pink, and Bella reflected that he must have the same horror of legs as the late, unlamented Lady Strickland. Though perhaps he was merely sensitive on her and Issie's behalf, because he was aware that some ladies felt the word "leg" should not be spoken in polite society.

He uncovered Issie's delicate little feet (which Bella secretly envied, as hers were not so dainty), and picked up first one foot, and then the other, gently squeezing them as he had her hands, and it was at this point that Bella feared Issie might not survive the examination, as she'd never seen her so agitated. Issie was clutching the bed, had her eyes squeezed shut, and looked as if she wished she could die, or at least disappear.

The doctor covered her feet and looked around the bedchamber, his gaze coming to rest on the stack of books on her bedside table. "Do you read a lot, Miss Grant?" he asked, as if it was an idle question.

"I do," Issie said, a little defensively. "I enjoy it."

The doctor smiled. "I enjoy reading myself. I wish I had more time for it."

Issie smiled radiantly back at him, her first smile since he'd entered the room, and the doctor blinked in surprise, as if he had just realized that Issie was an attractive young woman and not an insentient body.

"Do you have any other hobbies or interests?" he asked, though he had picked up one of Issie's books and was looking at it and didn't seem too concerned with her reply.

"I play the pianoforte and sketch a little, but haven't done much of those things since my mother died last year."

"How did your mother die?" the doctor asked.

"She had an apoplexy," Bella replied on Issie's behalf, as she had noticed Issie's voice was weak and breathless and she was worried she hadn't the strength to answer so many questions.

"My condolences," the doctor said, dipping his head in a polite bow. Issie murmured her thanks. "And so you spend most of your waking hours . . ." He placed the book down and looked directly at her.

"Reading," said Issie, with a defiant expression that made it clear she would not appreciate any criticism of her favorite hobby.

"These attacks," the doctor said, "are they frequent?"

"Recently they have been."

"She's never been strong," Bella interjected, "but the nervous attacks seem to have started since we came to town, and she was unable to keep an appointment just recently because she'd had one."

The doctor studied Issie a moment more in silence, and she began to pluck nervously at the bedcover. "You say your mother died last year. Have you been in mourning for her this entire time?" the doctor asked, and then continued before she could reply: "I suppose a better question would be: Have you been in the habit of going out or receiving visitors since her death?"

"No, not at all. It wouldn't be proper, since I was in mourning. You are probably my first real visitor in a year," Issie explained. "The only person that I've seen—other than servants—is my cousin"—she nodded in Bella's direction—"and my great-aunt, once I arrived in town."

"And did my visit cause an attack?" the doctor asked.

"Oh, yes," Issie said, nodding her head. "It was quite the most vigorous attack I've ever had. My heart is still palpitating quite fiercely," she said, looking up into his very un-doctor-like, far-too-handsome face, the sight of which was causing a strange fluttering in her abdomen, in addition to the one in her heart.

"I see," he said, and Bella wondered if he did, while Issie, whose symptoms were very different from those she'd ever before experienced, hoped that he did not.

Bella walked the doctor down the stairs and to the door, asking him what was wrong with her cousin.

"I cannot be certain," Dr. Jordan said. "There was a paper published a few years ago in which one of my colleagues reported a peculiar, and fatal, heart ailment he'd observed. I would hate to push Miss Grant into activity that would precipitate an attack, and it's even more of a risk since it sounds as if she has a family history of such things. However, I also wonder if her sudden nervous attacks are because she's become used to leading a solitary, sedentary life, and she's weak from lack of physical activity. She could also be experiencing anxiety over normal human interactions to which she's no longer accustomed. Especially as she's spent the preceding year isolated from society due to her mourning period."

"I suspect the same, Doctor, but I also fear pushing her into something that could prove damaging to her."

"I would advise against forcing her to do anything too vigorous, for now. I will call again in a week and see how she does. If you are able to get her out of bed and into a chair, that would be helpful. Don't be too ambitious, but it would be best if she does not become completely immobile."

Bella thanked the doctor and sent him on his way, and went back upstairs to talk to Issie. One thing had become very clear: Issie was in no condition to have her come-out. Bella, realizing that meant she must now agree to take her place, wasn't sure how she felt about the prospect. She suspected it might cause *her* to have a nervous attack, but then reflected that only noble, wealthy ladies were allowed to so indulge themselves, and that she'd be better off spending her time doing something more productive. So she went upstairs and began altering Issie's dresses, since it appeared she would be wearing them for the next eight weeks.

The following day, Bella found herself at the point of no return. Lady Dutton took her on morning calls and introduced her to all those present, even to a patroness of the exclusive club Almack's, as "Lady Isabelle." Bella realized that, even if she might have one day been forgiven for appearing at court and being presented to Queen Charlotte under a false identity, she would never be forgiven for misleading Lady Jersey, one of the queens of London society.

But even after she and Lady Dutton had returned home, Bella's trials weren't over, for they soon had a caller of their own.

The butler brought a card to Aunt Lucretia to see if she would receive the visitor, and once the lady had been able to decipher what it said, she immediately told the butler they were "at home to Lord Brooke."

The name meant nothing to Bella, but when the gentleman entered the room, Bella immediately recognized him as the very attractive man she'd practically assaulted at St. James's Palace.

She found her favorable impression of him hadn't been false or exaggerated, as now that she saw him again he was just as handsome as she'd remembered, even though his complexion was not fashionably pale, like those of the gentlemen she'd met since she'd arrived in town. No, this man had a healthy tan and looked as if he spent most of his time outdoors, rather than at the gaming or dining table. He wore his dark hair in the Titus cut, cropped closely at the back with the front swept forward, but the front pieces were not overly long and pomaded into curls like those of some who wore the style. She hoped he wouldn't say anything to Lady Dutton about their previous meeting, as she imagined she'd broken numerous rules, first by sneaking out of the queen's drawing room, then by colliding into Lord Brooke, and finally by staying to converse with him even though they hadn't been introduced. But when she met his gaze with a look of anxiety in her own, he smiled at her and winked, and she expelled a breath of relief before returning his smile.

After telling Lord Brooke he could be seated, Lady Dutton said, "I need not introduce you to Lady Isabelle, as your mothers accomplished that before their untimely passing. 'Tis a pity they're not here to see you two reunited."

This was an unwelcome surprise to Bella, and she was immediately overcome by panic. He had already been introduced to Issie? If so, he had to now know that Bella was a fraud. And why hadn't Issie told Bella she had a gentleman acquaintance in London?

"We were previously introduced, but I think it's been so long since our last meeting that Lady Isabelle has forgotten it altogether," Lord Brooke said, apparently assuming it was embarrassment over her failure to recognize him that was causing Bella's stricken silence.

"It *has* been a long time," Bella said, thinking that a safe thing to say as he'd said so himself. "I cannot recollect exactly; how long has it been?"

"It had to have been more than five years ago now, perhaps six. My mother died in 1813, and you and your mother visited Bluffton Castle some time before her death."

"Of course, now I remember." Bella actually did remember the occasion. Bella had been miserable at the time, as she had not been allowed to accompany Issie on a visit to a castle. Now she was very glad she had been left at home. "Though if it were that long ago I would have been practically a child, as I'm nineteen now," said Bella, who was actually twenty. But Issie was nineteen.

"Yes, you were still a child at our last meeting," Lord Brooke said, subjecting her to a piercing stare. "Which might explain why I find you so very different now from how I remember you."

"I'm not sure how to take that remark; is it an insult or a compliment?" Bella asked, so nervous that she was about to be ignominiously revealed as an impostor that she scarcely knew what she was saying.

"It is merely a statement of fact. If I said you'd changed for the better I'd be insulting you as a child, but since I do think you've become an extraordinarily lovely lady, I was obviously a callow fool who lacked the discernment necessary to appreciate the uncut diamond in my midst."

"That was a very pretty compliment and I thank you," Bella said, relaxing a little at his remark. It appeared he found Bella different from his recollections of Lady Isabelle, but that he didn't suspect she *wasn't* Lady Isabelle. "They could have used such diplomatic skills at the Congress of Vienna," she said with a pert smile, and he returned the smile with a knowing one of his own and a slight nod, as if acknowledging that, in trying to be tactful, the compliment he'd paid her was a little *too* flowery and bordered on the pompous.

"Lord Brooke is too much of a gentleman to involve

himself in such affairs," Lady Dutton said, breaking into their conversation. Bella and Lord Brooke exchanged a look of surprise at such an absurd statement, as those who participated in the peace negotiations in Vienna had been the premier gentlemen of the kingdom. Bella thought Lady Dutton must have been concerned that "Lady Isabelle" was about to display her bluestocking tendencies, and so she had forced a change of subject. But Bella wasn't too disappointed at Lady Dutton's interruption, as Lord Brooke's very observant, intelligent gaze had politely turned from Bella to his hostess, and it gave Bella a chance to compose herself. She was extremely relieved that he didn't realize that she was an impostor, and even further impressed at his ability to rescue her from her foolish blunders, conversationally or otherwise. But perhaps he was *too* smooth? Such a debonair, attractive, confident man must find it easy to turn the heads of naive young women like herself. She'd have to be on her guard around him, for more reasons than one.

However, Bella was very pleased when she arrived at her first ball and saw that Lord Brooke was present. She told herself that her pleasure was due to the fact that she was already acquainted with him and she knew so few people in London. That had to have been the reason for the leaping of her pulse when their eyes met and the spontaneous smile that rushed to her lips.

So glowing was her smile that Lord Brooke looked over

his shoulder as if to confirm it was directed at him. Then he bowed his head at her in acknowledgment, and returned the smile with an appealing one of his own, before crossing the room to where she and Lady Dutton stood.

He bowed to the ladies and greeted them before asking Bella to dance.

Bella happily accepted and, once they were on the floor, thanked him for asking her. "I know so few people, you see, and this is my first *real* ball. I would have been so disappointed if no one had asked me to dance."

Lord Brooke studied the expression of the lovely young woman who spoke so confidingly to him, unsure at first if she was indulging in false modesty in an attempt to win a compliment. Surely, she had to realize she need have no fear of joining the wallflowers. But judging by her expression she was being completely sincere, and he was struck once again by the depth of her charm. Never had he met a woman so vibrant and genuine, who gazed up at him with her whole heart shining from her eyes. He was grateful her sheltered upbringing had not irrevocably crushed her, as he had been afraid it would. Either Lady Strickland had not been able to stifle her natural spirit, or now that she was free from her mother's tyranny she was finally able to let her true personality blossom forth.

Nor was there any hint of the extreme shyness she'd shown when he'd seen her at court. "How did your presentation go?" he asked her, while they were waiting for the first couple to progress down the line. "Were you able to retreat from the royal presence without injuring yourself or others?"

She laughed. "No injuries, thank goodness; unless I injured you when I crashed into you so suddenly."

"Not a bit. And even if you had, I never complain when beautiful ladies throw themselves into my arms," Lord Brooke said, and Lady Isabelle did display some shyness then, as she looked down with a blush.

But she quickly recovered and, peeping mischievously up at him, said, "If it happens to you on such a frequent basis, then perhaps *I* was not the clumsy one." He laughed but had no time to reply as the dance separated them.

"Have you been living alone at Fenborough Hall since your mother's passing, or do you have other family?" Lord Brooke asked, when they were waiting again at the bottom of the set.

"My cousin lives with me. We grew up together and are more like sisters than cousins. She came to town with me as well, but her health doesn't permit her to go out in society."

"I am sorry she is not well enough to go out. Perhaps I could meet her the next time I call," Lord Brooke said, and though he meant what he said, he said it mostly to be polite. So he was surprised when Lady Isabelle looked startled and frowned. "Though if she's not able to receive guests, I completely understand," he hurried to add.

"Unfortunately she is not," she said, and looked so distressed that Lord Brooke assumed her cousin suffered from some sort of serious illness and that it would be best to change the subject. He asked Lady Isabelle about her interests and pastimes and was pleased to find she enjoyed riding.

"Perhaps we could ride together some morning," he suggested, and since she was new to society, she did not recognize this for the boon it was. The highly eligible Lord Brooke did not usually take nubile young ladies riding in Hyde Park for the world to see. "Of course, it's not quite as enjoyable in town as it is in the country, but it's the second-most agreeable form of exercise for a young lady having her come-out."

"The *second*-most? What is the first?"

"I'm surprised you have to ask," Lord Brooke said, just before he grasped her by both hands to lead her down the middle of the dancers and back again, doing so with such vigor and athleticism that Bella laughed from pure joy.

The dance ended shortly afterward, and when Lord Brooke returned her to Lady Dutton's side she was besieged by gentlemen with dance requests. Lord Brooke berated himself for his stupidity in not securing another dance with Lady Isabelle while he'd had the opportunity, but was able to gain Lady Dutton's permission to take her on a drive the next day, and so contented himself with that.

When she returned home Bella was too elated and excited to sleep, even after Nancy had helped her undress and left her alone in her darkened chamber. She wished Issie were awake so that she could recount every moment of that glorious evening. For the first time in her life she had truly been the "belle of the ball." But as soon as the thought crossed her mind she laughed at herself, both for her silly pun and for letting the attention go to her head. There would not have been a line of eager gentlemen begging to dance with her if she'd attended the ball as the obscure Arabella Grant. However, as Lady Isabelle, rich young heiress of noble birth, she was bound to be sought after.

And then all of her joyous feelings dissipated, replaced with deep misgivings about the imposture in which she'd agreed to participate.

She realized now that she had been very shortsighted. She should have considered the ramifications such a decision would have for *her* future, rather than merely Issie's. Because while she had argued, very reasonably, that such a pretense would hinder Issie's marital prospects, Bella now realized it even more disastrously affected her own.

It was suddenly clear to her that if she did meet a man she desired to marry or even have as a friend, such a relationship could never amount to anything now that she had presented herself under a false identity. Whereas if she had immediately told the truth to Lady Dutton and waited for Issie to improve in health, Bella might have met some of these same gentlemen and discovered whether they actually admired *her* and were not just attracted by Lady Isabelle's wealth and status. It was true that Bella would not have been invited to all the high-society events that Issie was, but she would have been allowed to attend *some* entertainments. And she could have promenaded or gone riding in the park with Issie, and through her have been introduced to the same persons she was meeting now, but as herself, the inconsequential, poor Miss Grant, not the noble, wealthy Lady Isabelle.

And what future was there for Bella if she didn't find a husband? She knew that Issie would always offer her a home but, as fond as she was of her cousin, Bella would never be content living the isolated and reclusive life that Issie genuinely enjoyed. Bella wanted to be married; she wanted children; she wanted the familial fondness and affection she'd been deprived of her entire life. It was true that Issie loved her—and Bella did not know what she would have done without that love in a life that had been barren of it—but it was a slightly selfish love, which required that Bella subordinate her own wants and needs in favor of Issie's. Bella recognized it wasn't Issie's fault that they'd fallen into such a pattern; it had started when Bella, the elder by one year, had designated herself her cousin's protector and tried to shield Issie from her autocratic mother. It was also a result of Bella being made to feel second-best by Lady Strickland from the moment she'd arrived at Fenborough Hall as a three-year-old and having no other option but to accept that role.

However, Bella's habit of giving in to Issie had now led her into this unfortunate situation, and she resolved to be firmer in the future. Though such a resolution was of no help at all in her present difficulties.

Because, while Bella had danced with several gentlemen

that evening whom she had found congenial, it was the impossibility of any future relationship with one gentleman in particular that was the cause of her current depression. She had felt a connection to Lord Brooke from the very start of their acquaintance, when she'd so clumsily bumped into him and he had so gallantly, and kindly, accepted the blame. As handsome as he undeniably was, she found his kindness even more appealing.

But it was folly to cry over spilt milk, and she couldn't reverse her ill-considered decision at this point. She'd only recently met Lord Brooke, they were barely acquainted, and now that she knew there was no possibility of a future with him, she could take measures to protect her heart. Surely, it would do no harm to enjoy a light flirtation with him and the other gentlemen she'd met, all of whom appeared more than eager to flirt with her. In fact, she was most likely flattering herself that any of them had any serious intentions toward her. Or would have had any, if they'd known who she really was. And, while Bella had not formed a distinct picture of the man she'd hoped to marry when she'd dreamt of a future family, an earl would have been the last man she would have envisioned, or desired. Living with Lady Strickland had made her wary of the nobility. She did not want to spend the next forty or fifty years of her life feeling inferior, as she had for the first twenty.

So she attempted to dismiss her anxious concerns and settled back into the plump feather pillow on her beautiful canopied bed. She would forget any foolish notion of forming a permanent attachment to a gentleman she met this season and just do her best to enjoy herself. This was a holiday the likes of which she'd never experienced before, and never would again.

It was unfortunate that the same could be said of the likelihood of ever meeting another man like Lord Brooke.

4

It had become a custom for the two girls to break their fast in their rooms, partly because they were able to spend some time alone together, but also because Bella had no desire to encounter Lord Dutton again over the poached eggs.

Bella was relieved to find that Issie's health had improved tremendously, and so Bella had encouraged her to make the short walk to her own more spacious chamber so that they could breakfast there. Keeping in mind Dr. Jordan's warnings, however, she was extremely considerate of Issie, helping her rise from bed and offering her an arm to lean on. But Issie seemed much stronger than she had a few days earlier when the doctor had called. Bella wondered if it could have been merely the *prospect* of her presentation that had sickened her so. Bella was definitely not an expert on the science of such a thing, but she had observed that the mind could exert a powerful influence on the body.

While they were eating, Bella confided in Issie some of the concerns that had troubled her the night before, but Issie was quick to dismiss them.

"I understand how you feel, Bella, but you'll have more than enough time for such things in the future, if you're still convinced you want to marry," Issie said. "You needn't rush into bondage now, just as we've achieved our freedom."

Bella wondered why and how Issie had formed such a negative opinion of marriage, as it was Issie's *father* who had been under the iron rule of his wife while he'd been alive and, as far as Bella knew, Issie had never witnessed firsthand a marriage where the woman had been in servitude to the man. But Bella was aware there were far more examples of that than the opposite, and so Issie must know it as well. Bella understood, too, why Issie wanted them to enjoy their independence a little longer. It was refreshing not to have to answer to anyone; not even Lady Dutton, whose chaperonage was surprisingly lax.

But even though Bella, like Issie, had no desire to rush into marriage, neither did she want to miss out on an opportunity that may never be presented to her again. "It's not that I want to marry immediately," she explained, "it's just that I've never met a gentleman as nice as Lord Brooke—"

"Lord Brooke!" Issie interrupted, before Bella could revise the measly description she'd given of him, as she'd just been about to do. Certainly, Lord Brooke was deserving of a more flattering accolade than "nice." But apparently Issie didn't think so.

"I don't know why you persist in admiring that man.

Didn't I tell you how haughtily he treated me when I visited him and his mother?"

"He was what, one-and-twenty at the time? He was probably just ill at ease," Bella said defensively. "And you were what, fourteen? How did you expect him to treat you? If he had paid you too much attention when you were so young that *would* have been strange. And you weren't old enough to be an astute judge of character, either. I told you how kind he was to me at our first meeting."

"You are very pretty, Bella. No doubt that influenced his behavior toward you." And from Issie's tone of voice it was obvious that Lord Brooke's preference for attractive females was another point against him in her view.

Bella tried her best to raise Lord Brooke in her cousin's esteem, but Issie was firm in her belief that he was not good enough for her dear cousin.

"Trust me, Bella. We'll go to Bath or Tunbridge Wells in a year or two, and you'll meet someone who makes Lord Brooke look paltry in comparison," Issie told her, and Bella wondered how Issie had managed to form such a negative impression of the man, and one the exact opposite of her own.

Later that day Bella discovered that she had not been immodest in declaring herself the "belle of the ball," if only in her thoughts, because more than one person had voiced the same opinion. And based on this widely pronounced sentiment, together with her assumed name, some London wit had christened her with the sobriquet "Lady Belle."

She first heard this new title when the gentlemen who had danced with her—along with some who had not successfully secured a dance—presented themselves in Lady Dutton's drawing room that afternoon for "morning" calls. There were even a few young ladies present, who had been brought by their mothers and chaperones in the hope that Lady Belle's popularity was somehow contagious.

Bella was completely overwhelmed by her reception from London society. While of course she had hoped to be liked and had greatly enjoyed the attention she'd received at her first ball, she hadn't expected, or wanted, to be the toast of the town. It would be much more difficult to keep up her masquerade while under such keen scrutiny.

But quoting another proverb to herself—*in for a penny, in for a pound*—she resolved to do her best to enjoy the attention. And such a resolution didn't prove at all difficult once Lord Brooke entered the room.

He was greeted warmly by many of those present, and Bella observed that he appeared to be well-liked. She only wished Issie was there to see it.

However, the other gentlemen were not as happy with him when, after a few minutes, he reminded Lady Dutton of her promise to allow Lady Isabelle to drive with him, and there were loud complaints that Lord Brooke was trying to cut them out with "Lady Belle."

Later, after they had made their escape and Lord Brooke had successfully navigated through the worst of the traffic, he asked Bella what she thought of her new nickname.

"I like it," Bella said, a little defiantly, hoping he wouldn't think her vain for admitting it. Perhaps it would have been more ladylike to have put on a modest facade.

But Lord Brooke didn't seem at all offended. "I like it, too. It's not only accurate," he said, darting an admiring glance at his companion, "but it also seems to fit you better than 'Isabelle.'" He then hurried to add: "Not that Isabelle's not a beautiful name. It is. But it seems a little too . . . formal, for you."

Bella thought it was funny that his statement held true whether applied to Issie or herself. Issie had only ever been called Isabelle by her mother. Even the servants had referred to her as "Lady Issie" whenever Lady Strickland had been out of earshot.

"No one calls me Isabelle," she said.

"You are called Belle, then?" he asked.

Bella heartily wished she had not continued this conversation. She had no desire to be known as "Issie" by this man; being called Isabelle had been difficult enough. She made a sudden decision to answer him truthfully, as herself. "Actually, my cousin, and those who know me best, call me Bella."

"Bella," he repeated, as if trying out the name, and Bella shivered, both in fear of what she'd just admitted and its possible ramifications, and at the sound of her pet name on his lips. "I wouldn't presume to call you that, however, as I am not one of those who knows you best. Yet," he added with a grin, and Bella wondered if she should view his words as a promise or a warning.

"I also haven't granted you permission to do so, *Lord*

Brooke," Bella reminded him. Though she would have gladly allowed him to call her Bella and dispense with her assumed title altogether if she didn't realize it would seem incredibly forward.

"Please, call me *my* lord Brooke," he said. "And I will call you *my* lady Bella."

"I hardly think that would be appropriate," Bella said, but she couldn't keep from smiling as she said it, and he didn't appear to take her half-hearted rebuke at all seriously. He had a teasing, boyish smile on his face as he exchanged glances with her, and Bella could not fathom how Issie had been so completely immune to his charm, even at fourteen. She realized that this was undoubtedly for the best, however, because it would have been far worse if Issie had become infatuated with him before Bella had had the opportunity to do so.

They entered Hyde Park just then, and she was grateful when Lord Brooke began explaining to her some of its features. Particularly since the sight that greeted her was an extraordinary one. Never in her life had she seen so many people gathered in one location. Or even at multiple times in multiple locations.

However, she later discovered that the thousands of people riding, driving, and perambulating through the park that day were only a fraction of the fifty thousand it was said congregated there on a Sunday when the weather was fine. She learned also that a Persian ambassador who visited London in 1809 claimed there had been at least one hundred thousand persons present on his excursion to Hyde Park.

(Though she suspected a tourist might be inclined to exaggerate, and wondered how he could have possibly counted them.)

But even though the park wasn't at its busiest at that particular moment, she was still surprised and a trifle overwhelmed by the crowds, and so was happy to ride silently beside Lord Brooke as she looked avidly about her. Until, that is, it occurred to her that such behavior marked her as an unsophisticated rustic.

When she grew conscious of her bad manners, she turned to Lord Brooke suddenly, an apology on her lips, but if he had felt that she was behaving rudely, his expression gave no indication of it. He was watching her with a smile, which made Bella feel slightly self-conscious. It was true that they were proceeding at a snail's pace so he had no need to pay strict attention to the horses, who were following the carriage in front of them, but Bella thought there must be many more interesting sights for him to turn his attention to. Perhaps he was jaded by it all, this not being his first visit.

"I apologize for gaping," Bella said, gesturing to the crowds around them, "but this is a new experience for me."

"It's quite all right. I'm well entertained." Bella frowned, thinking he was amused by her ignorance. He saw her expression and hurried to explain. "Your face is so expressive. I enjoy seeing London again for the first time, through your eyes."

Bella relaxed at his explanation and felt a little foolish that she had jumped to the conclusion he was observing her in a critical manner. Her experience with Lady Strickland had made her overly sensitive. "What is *your* opinion of London?" she asked him.

"I like to visit, but I prefer life in the country. I'm obliged to come to town because of my seat in the House of Lords, and I do enjoy a night at my club and even the occasional ball or lecture, but life feels more . . . purposeful in the country. Of course, I'm in a privileged position in that I inherited a productive estate, but the management of it is no small task." He exchanged nods with a gentleman passing by on horseback before asking: "What about you? How are you enjoying life in town as opposed to the country?"

"I have very little experience of town, but it's definitely superior thus far to the country," Bella replied, and was shaken by an involuntary shudder at the thought of her life at Fenborough Hall prior to her aunt's death.

Lord Brooke appeared as if he understood a great deal from that one sentence, and unfortunately decided to pursue the topic she would have avoided at all costs. "It was remiss of me, but I never expressed my condolences at the loss of your mother."

"Thank you," Bella said, but before she could turn the subject, he continued: "She and my mother were rather close, you know."

"Were they?" Bella asked, congratulating herself on the ambiguity of that reply.

"Perhaps 'close' is not the right word. It would be more accurate to say that they shared similar ambitions. But I imagine you know very well what I'm referring to, so I won't embarrass you by mentioning it. At least, not now, when we've only just become reacquainted." He smiled reassuringly at Bella, while looking at her in a way that seemed to imply they shared a great secret, and Bella smiled back, while hoping she appeared as if she knew what he was talking about. She resolved to ask Issie about it at the earliest opportunity.

"I didn't know your mother well; indeed, I hardly knew her at all, but it seemed to me that she was rather . . . domineering," Lord Brooke said, a little hesitantly.

"She was," Bella replied, though she wondered if it would have been wiser to prevaricate. Still, she'd resolved to tell the truth whenever possible, and she wouldn't lie about Lady Strickland. "She was not a very sympathetic person."

"My mother was not particularly motherly, either," Lord Brooke said, with a little shrug, as if it mattered naught to him, and Bella thought his mother must have been a very coldhearted woman, indeed, to neglect the bright, engaging child he must have been. "I think my sister suffered from her indifference more than I did, however."

"I had forgotten you have a sister," Bella said, as she had never heard Issie refer to her and knew that Issie must have met her rarely, if at all.

Lord Brooke immediately confirmed Bella's supposition. "I doubt you would have ever had the opportunity to meet. Lucy was twelve years my senior. She married at eighteen and started a family of her own soon after, so was not at

Bluffton Castle when you visited. I would have been very pleased to introduce you, but unfortunately she passed away two years ago."

"I am so sorry," Bella said, very sincerely, as she could tell he felt the loss deeply.

"Thank you. Despite the age difference, we were very close. That is why I did not suffer from my mother's neglect; Lucy amply filled that place, even though she was still a child herself when I was born," he said, with a reminiscent smile. "She was a widow when she died, and I am guardian to her two boys. The eldest is nineteen and inherited his father's estate, which thankfully is only twenty miles from my own, so I'm able to visit frequently."

"No wonder you feel like you lead a more purposeful life in the country. It sounds as if you have a great deal to keep you busy."

"Perhaps it was because Lucy had warned me of the pitfalls, but I was able to see that a pleasure-seeking lifestyle was ultimately unsatisfying. As I mentioned, I enjoy it occasionally, while not making it the center of my life." He stopped a little abruptly and looked at her with a self-mocking smile. "I sound like a complete and total prig, don't I? Here you are, enjoying your first London season, and I'm pontificating on the virtues of country living, like a vicar delivering a sermon."

"You didn't sound at all like that," Bella protested.

"Yes, but you just said that you prefer town, so it's rather pompous of me to try to persuade you to my point of view."

"You're doing no such thing! I am perfectly able to formulate my own views and opinions, and to remain true to them even though a persuasive gentleman might attempt to convince me otherwise," she said. Her light tone saved her from sounding overly severe, though Lord Brooke's quick glance made it obvious he understood the deeper implications of her words. She continued before he could reply: "While I *am* enjoying myself, I can see that once the novelty wears off, an endless round of parties and entertainment could quickly pall. And it's not the country that I dislike. In fact, if I had a life as you describe—with a sense of purpose and a place that felt like a *real* home—why, I have no doubt that I'd prefer living in the country as well."

"How would you describe a real home?" Lord Brooke asked.

"One in which there is fondness, and affection, and where every member of the household is valued. Where parents, instead of viewing their offspring as a burden to be disposed of in a way that brings financial reward, see them as a blessing and a gift. And one in which marriage is not entered into because of obligation or material considerations, but because there is true sympathy, respect, and . . . and love between the participants," she replied, her voice trailing off a little at the end, as she grew embarrassed at stating her opinions so straightforwardly in front of a gentleman she hardly knew. She was also aware that, for the class of people she was pretending to belong to, love was not a prerequisite for marriage. But then, chiding herself for feeling ashamed, even fleetingly, about something she believed in so strongly, she sat up straighter and looked him in the eye, though she smiled self-mockingly as she did so. "Now *I'm* the one who sounds as if I'm delivering a sermon."

"Not at all. I've never heard a clergyman speak so eloquently on such a subject, more's the pity," he told her, and her mock smile transformed into a genuine one, from relief that she hadn't offended him.

And it was very obvious that she had not. Lord Brooke was looking at her with such warm approval that she wished she could remember the exact words she'd said to elicit that response. "I must admit that I feared your mother's harsh treatment would crush your spirit, but now I believe it's had the opposite effect. You have a strength of character that's quite rare. And very admirable," he said softly, and she was moved by the compliment, and the look in his eyes, until she remembered that he was laboring under a false impression. He thought she was Lady Isabelle; that she was Lady Strickland's daughter. But still, even though she wasn't whom he believed her to be, she knew herself to be just as deserving of his praise as Issie. Rather than let her aunt's harsh treatment destroy her as it very well could have, she'd endured her many cruelties with fortitude and even protected Issie when she'd been able to do so.

Therefore, she graciously nodded her head in acceptance of his compliment and said, "Thank you, my lord." And then she grinned when she realized she had just claimed him as hers, after all. He smiled back in acknowledgment of what she'd inadvertently said, and the serious mood was broken.

Bella had had every intention of asking Issie about the meaning of Lord Brooke's cryptic comment regarding their mothers' "ambitions," but the lovely compliment he'd given her had caused her to completely forget that earlier part of their conversation. While she had become used to admiring remarks on her appearance since coming to town—and was inclined to dismiss most of them, for what rich, eligible young lady wasn't considered beautiful?—she had received scant praise in the twenty years before her London debut. Lord Brooke was the only person she could recall, other than a favorite governess whom Lady Strickland had dismissed, who had complimented her on her character.

Another reason it had slipped her mind was because the social whirl kept her so busy in the days following her and Lord Brooke's drive in the park that she rarely saw Issie except for their breakfasts together, and Bella had even missed a few of those. But when it was time for Dr. Jordan to call again, Bella was careful not to schedule any other activities so that she could be present to chaperone Issie.

Bella quizzed Issie about her health before the doctor arrived, asking her if she'd had any recurrence of the palpitations she'd experienced when they'd first arrived in town.

"Not really, no. I do seem to be somewhat stronger. But I'm sure it's because I have been resting, and my poor nerves have not been subjected to the rigors of the London season," she hurried to explain, probably so that Bella couldn't complain that their exchange of identities had been unnecessary.

And once again, Issie's expression and tone of voice as she referred to the "London season" displayed such an aversion that an unbiased observer might have assumed that it involved being pilloried in Charing Cross, rather than being feted and wooed by the most eligible gentlemen in London. Bella realized, however, that Lady Strickland's constant criticism had greatly undermined Issie's confidence and that is why she was so apprehensive about appearing in public. To Issie, a London season *was* comparable to being placed in the stocks. "I know you don't wish to be introduced into society, Issie, but a short walk in the park would do you no end of good."

But just the suggestion of such a thing caused Issie to clutch her chest and shake her head. "No, Bella, I wouldn't want to have a relapse."

Bella didn't argue the point, as she hoped that Dr. Jordan would be able to influence Issie to participate in some moderate exercise. Especially since his initial theory—that Issie had grown weak through lack of activity—appeared to have been proven true. Bella knew, too, that the suddenness of Lady Strickland's death had exacerbated Issie's fears, so that she was now confusing her body's natural reaction to exertion after months of inactivity with the symptoms of an impending apoplexy. However, Bella did not feel Issie was in danger of meeting her mother's fate. The late Lady Strickland had become enraged easily and frequently, and such violent emotions had probably overtaxed her heart. Issie, on the other hand, never flew into rages or threw fits of temper. Although Bella did fear for her cousin's health if she did not start eating regularly and engaging in physical activity.

Therefore, shortly before the doctor's arrival, Bella was quite surprised when she had to stop Issie from doing too *much*.

Issie had frantically knocked on Bella's door to ask her if she had altered all the gowns that had been purchased for her season.

"Not all of them, no," Bella replied. "Was there one in particular you wanted to wear?" She was careful to keep her voice and expression neutral, and though she dearly wanted to tease Issie about trying to look her best for the handsome doctor, she restrained herself with great difficulty from doing so.

"I believe there was a sprigged muslin," Issie said, but she had already gone into Bella's dressing room and started looking through the gowns herself. "This one!" she pronounced excitedly, pulling it down and showing it to Bella.

"It hasn't been altered. You should keep it," Bella said. But Issie had already rushed out of the room with the dress, and Bella was not even sure she'd heard her.

She followed Issie to her room and found her undoing the ties of the simple white morning gown she'd worn at breakfast. "I'm glad you came, Bella. You can help me. I rang for Nancy, but I'm worried the doctor will come before she does," Issie said, the last part of her sentence nearly inaudible as her voice was muffled by the dress she was pulling over her head.

Bella quickly helped Issie change clothes, as Issie had left it to the very last minute and the doctor could be announced at any time. Apparently, she'd had second thoughts about what she'd been wearing, and Bella felt she was right to choose something other than unrelieved white, which made her appear even more pale and sickly than she was.

Having helped Issie into her dress, Bella tried to lead her back to bed, but Issie resisted Bella's guiding arm and ran to the vanity to look in the mirror and fuss with her hair. This was when Bella began to fear Issie might be overdoing things. "Issie, please! You'll exhaust yourself before the doctor arrives. You look very pretty."

Issie was pulling curls out from under her lace cap while peering anxiously at herself in the mirror. "I'm still rather pale." Then, looking at her cousin as if they were co-conspirators in a crime, she whispered: "Do you have any . . . *rouge*?"

But before Bella could answer yea or nay (and she did resort to the rouge pot on occasion, though always very faintly and discreetly), there was a knock at the door followed by Nancy's voice. "The doctor's here, mislady." (Nancy had taken to addressing them both with a word that was a garbled combination of "miss" and "milady" and spoken in a lowered tone so that it was even more difficult to decipher. Bella thought this was very clever of her.)

Issie froze in shock, but Bella told her not to worry. Going over to the door, she said in a raised voice: "Don't bring him up just yet, Nancy."

She then heard Nancy tell the doctor to wait a moment

and the murmur of a masculine reply, and Bella realized Nancy might not be as clever as she thought.

Rolling her eyes, Bella went back to Issie, who had run over to lie on the bed, her back propped against a pillow and her legs stretched out in front of her. Bella helped her tuck her dress neatly around her legs. "Should you cover my feet with the blanket or do you think he will . . . touch them again?" Issie asked Bella, and turned such a fiery red that she had no need of rouge, after all.

"I'll cover them," Bella said, as she could sense Issie was about to have palpitations and wanted to delay them for as long as possible.

She covered Issie with the blanket and arranged a few of her nut-brown curls so that they framed her face. She stood back to survey her handiwork and then smiled at her cousin. "You look lovely," Bella told her. Issie returned the smile and Bella went to the door to let the doctor in.

He greeted Bella without looking at her, his gaze immediately going to the young lady in the bed. Issie was still faintly smiling and her cheeks were tinged with the remnants of a blush. Her eyes shone from her unaccustomed exertion (or perhaps from nerves) and her sprigged muslin was an excellent choice, as the blue floral motif embroidered on the gauzy white cotton exactly matched her eyes and made them appear even more luminous.

"Why, you are looking *exceedingly* well!" the doctor exclaimed, returning Issie's smile. This caused Issie to blush even more, and Bella thought again that it was a good thing they hadn't painted her cheeks. "How are you feeling?" he asked.

"Somewhat better," Issie replied.

"Your palpitations have decreased in frequency?" he asked.

"Yes, though my nerves are still a little . . . agitated," she said, staring up into his concerned, attentive gaze and feeling quite agitated at that very moment.

The doctor turned to address Bella. "I think that the supposition we discussed about her weakness being caused by lack of activity is probably correct." Bella nodded her agreement, but Issie's smile disappeared and her brow furrowed at this remark. The doctor turned back to Issie. "I have a prescription for you."

Issie did not look at all excited by this prospect.

"I want you to join your cousin on at least one outing every other day. It could be a simple one, like a trip to the shops or a walk in the park, but you need to increase your physical activity."

"I went shopping when I first arrived in town and it was extremely deleterious to my health," Issie said. But perhaps the doctor was accustomed to resistance to his suggestions, because his smile didn't waver.

"I don't mean the type of strenuous shopping that you ladies indulge in when you come to town, where you're fitted for a whole new wardrobe," he said, his eyes flitting over Issie's very modish gown, "but just a quick jaunt to buy ribbons, or even just to look in the shop windows. Something to get you out of the bed, and out of the house."

"I've read that the air in London is quite noxious and harmful. You really think it would be good for me to spend more time out of doors in this rank city?" Issie protested.

"It's true that country air would be more salubrious, but since you are not presently in the country, town air will have to suffice."

Issie made no verbal response, but it was obvious that she was skeptical of the doctor's "prescription." Dr. Jordan exchanged an amused glance with Bella, before trying another tack.

"You are a well-read young lady, Miss Grant. Surely, you wish to explore the place of which Wordsworth wrote:
'Earth has not any thing to show more fair:
Dull would he be of soul who could pass by
A sight so touching in its majesty:
This City now doth, like a garment, wear
The beauty of the morning; silent, bare.'"

"Wordsworth held one opinion of London; Johnson held another," Issie replied, sitting up straighter in bed, before quoting:
"'Prepare for death, if here at night you roam
And sign your will before you sup from home.'"

Bella wanted to chuckle at Issie's quote but restrained herself, as she did not want to undermine the doctor's attempts to persuade her cousin that an outing in London would not prove fatal.

"Yet Johnson was later quoted as saying: 'When a man is tired of London, he is tired of life; for there is in London all that life can afford,'" the doctor replied.

Issie was silent for a moment, her brow wrinkled in thought. She then said excitedly, "What about William Cowper? He wrote about London:

'Rank abundance breeds,

In gross and pampered cities, sloth and lust

And wantonness and gluttonous excess.'"

"Cowper was practically a monk"—Issie's eyes grew large at such heresy—"but there was some truth in what he said," Dr. Jordan conceded, and Issie breathed a sigh of relief.

Bella was immensely entertained by this exchange, but wasn't sure who had emerged victorious, or what it was that they had won. "So, was anything decided by that?" she asked.

"I've decided it's a great pity that such an intelligent young woman hides herself away, when she'd be an asset to any gathering," Dr. Jordan replied.

Issie looked down in embarrassment, her expression conflicted. She was obviously flattered by his description of her, but just as obviously had no desire to leave the safety of her bedchamber.

"Perhaps if you were to accompany her on her first outing, Doctor," Bella suggested innocently. "Just as a precaution, of course, in case she suffered a relapse."

"I am very busy . . ." he said, but seeing the disappointment Issie could not fully conceal, he continued, "but I think I could carve out some time, if Miss Grant were to agree to it."

"She agrees," Bella said quickly. "Perhaps we could take

a trip to Ackermann's. I must confess I've been desirous of making a visit there myself."

Issie's eyes lit up at the choice of destination, and she was silent while Bella and the doctor settled upon an afternoon a week later. Obviously, Issie could not go unchaperoned, so Bella would accompany them. Though she resolved to leave them poring over the books while she perused the most recent caricatures and art prints.

In anticipation of this outing, Bella was able to talk Issie into going up and down the stairs multiple times in the days that followed, and was relieved that, rather than killing her as Issie had felt it might, the exercise had given her a slight glow. Or perhaps thoughts of Dr. Jordan were causing that. Either way, Bella felt the good doctor had more than earned his fee, and she was looking forward to observing him and Issie together on their upcoming excursion.

5

After their drive together in the park, Bella's friendship with Lord Brooke, which had appeared to be flourishing, cooled a little. This was because Bella—who felt she had let down her guard with him more than was prudent—began limiting her interactions with him. She had to protect not only her real identity, but also her heart, and she had to avoid intimate conversations with Lord Brooke if she was to accomplish both. So while she still danced with him at the occasional ball, she forced herself to decline his other invitations, even though she dearly wanted to accept.

She couldn't congratulate herself that she had fooled him as to her reasons, however. On one morning call, after she'd told him she was otherwise engaged and couldn't ride with him the next day, he gave her a quizzical look and she was forced to drop her gaze for fear he read her too well.

"Poor Lady Belle. Did I rush things?" he asked softly. "How gauche of me. Perhaps I *am* the clumsy one."

She looked up at that, and was relieved to see he hadn't appeared to take offense at her refusal, as he was smiling at her. But perhaps she shouldn't have rejoiced too much, as his smile was a knowing one. It was as if he fully understood what she was attempting to do and believed that it would be just a matter of time before she dropped her defenses.

So, in a further attempt at protection, she made other, safer acquaintances. And one friendship in particular was progressing at a rapid pace.

This was with a Miss Adams, whom Bella had met in the ladies' retiring room the night of her very first ball. The young lady had looked so scared and out of place that Bella had spoken encouragingly to her, not realizing that such encouragement would cause the lady to follow Bella around like a devoted puppy. Whenever Bella was not dancing, Miss Adams was by her side. This meant that Miss Adams was the recipient of quite a few dance requests from gentlemen who had not been fortunate enough to secure a dance with Bella. Which would have been an excellent reason in itself for her to strategically place herself at Bella's shoulder.

However, Bella quickly discovered that poor Miss Adams, or Catherine, as she insisted Bella call her, was not crafty enough to devise such a ploy. She reminded Bella of Issie in that she was ill at ease among strangers, and bullied by a strong-willed female. The female in her case was a Mrs. Mullins, a hired chaperone, who was quick to encourage her protégé to pursue a friendship with Lady Belle, the most popular young lady of the social season.

Because of Catherine's resemblance to Issie, Bella couldn't resist the urge to mother Catherine as well, and she soon felt the same fond protectiveness toward her as she did her cousin.

But even though she reminded Bella of Issie in character and situation, she was nothing like her in appearance. Catherine was round where Issie was thin, olive of complexion where Issie was pale, and had dark eyes and hair as opposed to Issie's pale blue eyes and light brown hair. Catherine also seemed to be in robust health, and romped about the ballroom in a manner that made her chaperone wince at the indelicacy, and caused Bella to smile at seeing her new friend enjoying herself.

Bella was glad, too, that Catherine was not as opposed to outdoor exercise as Issie was and, since Bella had turned down Lord Brooke's invitation, she made plans to ride with her new friend in the park. It was during this excursion that Catherine told Bella why it was she admired her so much.

"You're so sophisticated; you have such *presence*, while I'm a complete fraud," Catherine said, blowing a piece of hair out of her eyes in a gesture that would have made her chaperone shudder.

Bella winced at the word "fraud," but from Catherine's expression, it was obvious she'd intended no irony. "I'm not sure I understand. In what way are you a fraud?" Bella asked.

"Promise me you won't tell," Miss Adams said, looking over her shoulder to ensure their privacy, as if someone could have possibly snuck up and eavesdropped on a conversation that was taking place on the back of a moving horse.

"I promise," Bella said, smiling a little at Catherine's dramatics, as they reminded her of times when she and Issie had sworn each other to secrecy over some childish indiscretion.

"Our family's fortune comes from . . . trade," she said, before again sweeping the vicinity with a fearful glance.

"How shocking!" Bella said, smiling broadly to make it obvious she was joking. But apparently it was not obvious to Miss Adams.

"I know," she said sadly. "Mrs. Mullins made me swear never to betray my origins. When asked I'm to tell people I'm connected to the Adamses of Hampshire. They are a very genteel family, who would not even *think* of involving themselves in manufacturing. And it's not a lie, we are very distantly connected, though I would not call us a *branch* of the family. We are more like a twig." She paused, swallowed, and said quickly, as if she could not bear to conceal the truth: "Really, more like a sprout. Perhaps I shouldn't have told you—Mrs. Mullins says if it became known, no decent man would marry me—but I felt I could trust you with my secret."

"Of course you can, but I do not feel you need worry unduly over such a thing. You're a very kind and amiable young lady, and those are the qualities a *true* gentleman will be looking for in a wife."

Catherine appeared flummoxed by this statement, and it was the only time her eyes did not glow with the unconditional adoration Bella had grown accustomed to seeing directed at her. But after a moment the confused furrow on Catherine's brow disappeared and she smiled at Bella, the admiration returning to her gaze. "That's easy for you to say; you probably can't even comprehend what it's like for the rest of us. You're '*Lady Belle.*'" She pronounced the title reverentially, as if Bella were the Queen of England.

"So I am," said Bella, with a sigh.

Of the many gentlemen Bella had met since coming to London, there were two whom she would occasionally accept invitations from, as she'd taken a liking to both, and felt neither was in danger of mistaking a casual friendship for anything more. She also did not feel her own heart was in danger, as she did when around Lord Brooke.

The first, Mr. Charles Peckham, was only a year or two older than Bella and was also enjoying his first London season. She felt sure he was paying court to her because it was the fashion to do so, and not because he had any serious intentions. He was a cheerful, portly young man who dressed in the prevailing style that season of high cravats and extremely tight-fitting breeches, jackets, and waistcoats. This had the effect of emphasizing his plumpness rather than the opposite, and his buttons always looked to be under great strain. So it was no great surprise when on one occasion while he and Bella were dancing, the inevitable occurred and a button popped off.

The button was made of mother-of-pearl and was part of a matched set, so Mr. Peckham was extremely loath to lose it and spent the rest of their dance trying to locate it, to the detriment of his dancing, which was not of the highest caliber under the best of circumstances. Bella, who was at first embarrassed to have her partner keep her consistently off-step, eventually saw the humor in the situation, and began matching his steps as he looked for the button, improvising along the way. But when Mr. Peckham finally found the button and bent to retrieve it, she realized a disaster was bound to occur when the next couple turned and tripped over his hunched figure. And perhaps the next couple after that, and so on. In an attempt to avert the catastrophe, she called Mr. Peckham's name and begged him to rise. However, either he could not hear her over the music or he was too slow to respond, and Bella winced when the debacle she'd foreseen inevitably occurred.

Thankfully, no one was seriously hurt and Mr. Peckham retrieved his button. And, while that set came to an abrupt end, the next began after only a slight pause. (Though a few of the unfortunate dancers who had collided with Mr. Peckham had to leave the floor in order to check the integrity of their own buttons or laces, or both.)

Bella had hoped Mr. Peckham would learn from this experience that he should change tailors (or at least change the measurements his tailor was using), but this did not appear to be his primary concern. After he'd made what apologies he could and escorted Bella from the floor, he turned to her in dismay. "'Pon my soul, I did not know what to do. If I hadn't picked up the button someone might have tripped on it," he explained earnestly. Bella thought to herself that a man's stationary, crouching body was a much larger stumbling block than a button, but was too kind to express that aloud. "And, of course, I had those buttons designed specifically for this ensemble." He waved a hand proudly over his outfit, obviously inviting Bella to comment on it.

"They match your pearl stickpin very nicely," she said, and this satisfied him for a moment and he smiled, before the realization of the extent of his faux pas finally began to penetrate.

"I beg your pardon; that was inexcusable of me. It must have been quite . . ." He couldn't think of the appropriate word and took a deep gasp of air. Bella wondered if the tightness of his cravat was affecting his ability to breathe, or possibly preventing the flow of blood to his brain. "You'll probably never dance with me again; I made such a fool of myself," he said, with a hangdog expression. And Bella, who should have also learned a lesson from the mishap, heard herself saying: "Nonsense, I'd be pleased to dance with you again, Mr. Peckham."

When he beamed at her in response, she was happy she'd been able to cheer the poor fellow. But when he requested another dance that same evening, she was even happier to be able to tell him truthfully that her card was full.

Still, when he wasn't losing his accoutrements and turning the entire dance floor topsy-turvy, she found him enjoyable, undemanding company.

The second gentleman she'd allowed into her inner circle was totally different in appearance and character. Sir Roger Mann was taciturn and serious, and older than most of her suitors, as he was in his mid-thirties, at least. Like Mr. Peckham, she suspected Sir Roger had no real interest in marriage, especially since he'd reached such an advanced age and was still a bachelor. But though he didn't say much, what he said was always to good effect, and the few words he did use could usually surprise a laugh out of her. He was also a careless dresser, though somehow appeared more stylish than poor Mr. Peckham, who was so very à la mode.

After the incident with the button, her next dance was with Sir Roger, who offered to take her for refreshments instead. "I imagine you're peckish after your dance with Peckham," he said, straight-faced, and Bella, suppressing a giggle in case Mr. Peckham was still within earshot, said that she was not at all hungry, but that she was quite thirsty. While they were in the refreshment room Miss Adams appeared at her side.

"There you are," she said triumphantly, as if Bella had purposely hidden from her and Catherine had accomplished a great feat in finding her. "I was so concerned for you. How dare Mr. Peckham treat you in such a manner. He caused such a spectacle! I hope you refuse to dance with him from this point forward. Perhaps you can claim your card is full, since it would be impolite to refuse outright."

"It was unfortunate, but ultimately no real harm was done," Bella said in soothing tones, as Catherine seemed much more upset than she was herself. "Sir Roger, you are acquainted with Miss Adams, are you not?" She knew that he was, as she had previously introduced them. But Bella was unsure if he recalled Catherine's name and wanted to give him a hint. She also wanted to divert Catherine's attention from Mr. Peckham.

The two exchanged a bow and curtsy and murmured each other's names, but before any more conversation could take place, Lord Brooke entered the room, also in search of Bella.

"It's our dance, I believe, Lady Belle," he said, and Bella agreed that it was, and turned to thank Sir Roger for the refreshments. He merely nodded in response but, seeing Catherine's dark eyes turned upon him in hopeful expectation, asked her to dance with him. The foursome left the refreshment room, Bella and Lord Brooke walking ahead of the other couple.

"You will be relieved to know that I tested the integrity of all of my buttons in anticipation of my dance with you," Lord Brooke murmured to Bella.

She giggled, but quickly became serious. "Poor Mr. Peckham," she said, "is he never to live this down?"

"You're quite generous to be worried about *him*. Most ladies would be angered by the incident, and rightly so."

"Well, I am not one to fly up into the boughs for such a paltry reason as that," Bella said. As undignified and gauche as Mr. Peckham's behavior had been, Bella felt it paled in comparison to some of the vices that were tolerated among London society's high-class members. She'd come to realize that manners were prized more than morality by this elite group, and found their outrage over such innocent missteps hypocritical. At times she felt she'd gladly retire her position as "Lady Belle" when the season came to its end, she'd become so disillusioned with the so-called nobility.

But moments later, as she waltzed with Lord Brooke and his dark, intelligent eyes peered deeply into her own as if he could see beyond the false identity she'd assumed and into her very soul, she perversely wished the season would *never* end.

"You seem too good to be real," Lord Brooke said as they danced.

Bella's heart leapt at his words, but it calmed as soon as it occurred to her that he was merely responding to her remark about not becoming upset at Mr. Peckham, and she was able to answer him in a steady tone. "Because I forgave Mr. Peckham? If you must know, I feel sorry for the man, though you must never tell him I said so. However, if *you* pulled such a stunt on me, I'd be less inclined to forgive you so readily. But then, I could never envision you acting in such a way." In contradiction of what she'd just said, she had to suppress a giggle at the mental image her words had conjured up of Lord Brooke bumbling about the dance floor in search of a button.

"How very interesting," Lord Brooke said, his brow furrowed in contemplation. "Should a man seek to inspire pity in a woman, then? It sounds a terrible fate to me, though it did cause you to grant Mr. Peckham forgiveness, which makes me think perhaps there are advantages I'd never before considered. But would a woman seriously consider the suit of a man she *pitied*?"

Bella paused to consider his question. "Some women would, perhaps. It does lead to a softening of emotions. Perhaps in time it would deepen into affection."

"Would *you* marry a man you felt sorry for?"

Bella considered for the first time what her life would be like if she were married to Mr. Peckham, whom she found enjoyable company, but only because his antics did not reflect on her. At least in her opinion they did not, as she was not his relation, or his wife. But if he were her husband? That would be a far different matter. "I highly doubt I'd ever marry a man I pitied. I think it would be difficult to have the . . . proper respect for such a man," Bella finally answered.

"Then I suppose I should be glad you don't pity me," Lord Brooke said with a smile. And it was so devastatingly attractive, that smile, and had such a dangerous effect on Bella, that she felt *she* was the one who should be pitied.

The next day was the one appointed for the Ackermann's excursion, and once again Bella felt Issie might be a little *too* worked up. Bella tried to calm her before the doctor arrived to escort them, but gave it up as a lost cause, and hoped the increased excitement would be beneficial for Issie's health rather than the opposite.

The doctor had arranged to come at three o'clock, which Bella thought was an ideal time, as the day's callers had already come and gone, and hopefully the members of the *ton* would be on the strut in Hyde Park or dressing in preparation for their evening's activities. She supposed it didn't matter who saw her and Issie together—other than Lord Brooke, who might recognize Issie if he saw her again—but she wanted to avoid having to make any unnecessary introductions. She hated hearing herself presented as Lady Isabelle, and it would only increase her unease to have to introduce Issie to her London acquaintances as "Miss Grant."

She wondered if it would have been wiser to have chosen a more obscure location for Issie's first public outing. While Bella hadn't yet been there herself, she had heard Ackermann's was extremely popular with the crème de la crème of London society, who felt their presence at this emporium of arts and culture proved that they were just as refined and sophisticated as they purported to be.

Rudolph Ackermann had immigrated to London from Germany to work as a coach-maker before deciding he'd prefer to make prints and publish books instead. He opened first a drawing school and printshop before expanding into the "Repository of Arts" at 101 Strand, their destination that afternoon. At this shop one could purchase paintings, artists' supplies, caricatures and prints, as well as books, many of them illustrated.

Bella and Issie had only become aware of Mr. Ackermann after coming to London, as Lady Dutton had a subscription to his popular periodical: *The Repository of Arts, Literature, Commerce, Manufactures, Fashions and Politics.* Bella's favorite parts were the fashion plates and the illustrations of interior decoration and furnishings. Issie was interested in the literature, of course, but she also had a talent for sketching, which she hadn't indulged in since her mother's death, and Bella hoped a visit to Ackermann's might encourage her to take up this activity again.

The doctor arrived at the time promised, and the three of them left in Lady Dutton's coach, which Bella had secured permission to use. Dr. Jordan was not wealthy enough to keep a carriage, and Bella did not want to put him to the expense of hiring one. Issie, never having had to think about money, had not even considered these details. Bella reflected again on the unusual upbringing that Issie had experienced, one where she'd been both spoiled and deprived. If Issie were to follow the doctor's advice and break out of her self-imposed isolation, Bella thought she would greatly benefit not only physically but emotionally as well.

Dr. Jordan appeared ill at ease during the drive, as did Issie. Bella thought both were probably uncomfortable spending time together outside of their professional relationship. So Bella bore most of the conversational burden. The trip seemed interminable for that reason, though Dr. Jordan eventually began pointing out some of the sights from the window as they neared Ackermann's. One interesting sight was the newly constructed Waterloo Bridge, just completed the year before.

"It was called 'the noblest bridge in the world' by the Italian sculptor Canova and cost a million pounds to build," Dr. Jordan told them. "Perhaps we should descend from the carriage, in order to see it better," he suggested, as very little could be seen of it from their vantage point. Bella thought Issie might worry about the crowded streets or the strenuous walk, but she uttered not a word of protest. The doctor called to the coachman, and when the carriage stopped, he stepped out. He then assisted Bella to descend by giving her his arm, but when Issie prepared to exit, he grasped her by the waist and lifted her down, apparently concerned the descent would be too much for her. Issie was, in fact, breathing heavily, but Bella did not think it was due to poor health. She appeared very flustered to find herself, even briefly, in the doctor's arms.

After releasing Issie, he held out an arm for both her and Bella to take, but it was obvious his primary concern was for Issie, and he took slow steps through the crowded streets, positioning himself slightly in front of her as if to protect her from any buffeting by the crowds.

Bella thought it was a good thing Issie had worn a poke bonnet that day, as it functioned almost like the blinders worn by a high-spirited horse, and prevented her from being overwhelmed by the large number of people. Or maybe it was the doctor's presence that accomplished it. Whatever the reason, Issie was surprisingly calm in the few minutes it took the doctor to find a more isolated location with a view of the bridge.

It was a mild spring day and the river glistened in the afternoon sun. The Waterloo Bridge was as glorious an architectural accomplishment as it had been reputed to be, and its arches and columns provided the perfect frame for the skyline of London that rose up behind it. When Bella saw the trembling smile on Issie's lips, she realized Issie was experiencing the same joie de vivre that she was. If so, it was probably one of the first times in Issie's life that she hadn't experienced such a thing vicariously, through the pages of a book.

"I can understand the sentiments Wordsworth expressed about the city much better now," Issie said softly to the doctor, referencing their former argument about the virtues of London and tacitly conceding the point to him, and he smiled at her in response.

Bella felt somewhat de trop, but since she couldn't disappear she remained as quiet as possible, while the doctor pointed out London landmarks to the surprisingly eager young lady at his side. When he gestured at Somerset House, which was not far from where they stood, Issie's expression became almost reverential.

"I have read—that is, is it true that the artwork of the Royal Academy members is on display at Somerset House and it is open to the public?"

"It is. It opens every year on the first Monday in May. Just yesterday, it so happens," the doctor replied.

Issie turned impulsively to Bella. "Oh, Bella, is it possible we could go there, instead of Ackermann's? I've always wanted to see an exhibition there."

Bella was so happy that Issie was enjoying herself—that she was fully engaged in an activity instead of lying morosely in bed—she would have agreed to go on a tour of Newgate Prison if Issie had desired it. "I'd be delighted to visit the Royal Academy," Bella said. "We can always visit Ackermann's another time. That is, if the doctor agrees it wouldn't overtax your strength. I imagine it's more strenuous an excursion than the one we'd planned."

Both ladies turned to look at Dr. Jordan in silent inquiry, but he did not immediately respond. He had an expression of indecision on his face, and Bella assumed it was because he *was* concerned about whether Issie had enough stamina for such a thing. "The stairs to the main picture gallery are quite steep, and it's a very extensive collection. Even I was fatigued at the end of my last visit," he said, and Issie's face fell, but she nodded in resignation. Her woebegone look was very affecting, however, and it appeared Dr. Jordan was unable to resist it. "Then again, there are benches if you find it necessary to rest, and we could always leave if you become overtired," he added, and Bella felt he was in danger of spoiling Issie as badly as she did.

They made their way there in the carriage, even though Dr. Jordan and Bella could have easily walked the short distance to Somerset House. Neither wanted to squander Issie's limited strength before they even began their tour, and there was still a staircase to ascend.

When they arrived the doctor insisted on paying their admission, a shilling each, though Bella paid an additional shilling to obtain a catalogue of the works currently on display.

She was shocked at the length of the catalogue: sixty-five pages! But after they'd entered the Great Room and she saw the stacks upon stacks of paintings, covering every inch of the wall from floor to (very high) ceiling, she was no longer surprised at the length of the brochure.

Bella had been so pleased at Issie's interest in touring the Royal Academy she hadn't even considered the fact that there was bound to be even more of the fashionable set present there than there would be at Ackermann's. She was also too engrossed in keeping a concerned watch on Issie when they first arrived to think about anything else. Bella knew Issie's anxiety around strangers was real, and the rooms were *extremely* crowded.

However, the poke bonnet was again proving to be a handy contrivance, as it was narrowing Issie's gaze to the painting in front of her and blocking the hordes of people from her sight. And the doctor was also quite helpful; if Issie became anxious he would instruct her to take deep breaths, then distract her attention by pointing out a notable piece of art, all while shielding her slight figure from the crowd with his own.

Bella breathed a sigh of relief and felt she could finally shift her own attention to the exhibit rather than her cousin. She stepped a few paces away in order to look more carefully at a painting titled *The Gossip*. It was then that she realized she was receiving attention herself.

"It's the Lady Belle," she heard a gentleman say, and a few heads swiveled in her direction.

"Lady Belle," she heard again and ignored it. Then someone said: "Bella."

She turned in surprise when she heard her name, her *actual* name, and saw that it was Lord Brooke. He smiled ruefully when their gazes met and stepped closer. "I beg your pardon, I know that was impertinent of me, but I wanted to distinguish myself from the rest of your admirers."

She felt her cheeks grow hot with embarrassment and made a dismissive gesture, but he didn't appear to see it. "Who accompanied you here?" he asked, with a frown of concern. When Bella turned to look for Issie, she saw that she and Dr. Jordan were no longer standing nearby, but were both seated at a bench in the middle of the room. Bella realized that it looked as if she were completely unchaperoned.

"I'm here with my cousin," she replied, and then wished she'd thought of something else to say, as Lord Brooke would naturally ask to be presented to her.

"Your cousin? Then her health has improved?"

"Somewhat. Though I think this visit may have been a little too much for her. She is resting at the moment," Bella said, waving a hand in the direction of the benches. She did not think his memory of Issie was so strong that he would recognize her as Lady Isabelle from thirty feet away, and really, only the back of her bonnet was visible. But she did not want him requesting an introduction, so she turned frantically to the nearest painting and stepped toward it before she even had time to see what it portrayed, she was so intent on distracting him. "This piece is quite interesting," she said.

Then she blinked, as she found herself confronted with a large painting of scantily clothed women—nymphs?— cavorting on the seashore. On either side of it hung portraits of various noblemen's favorite pets: a terrier, a spaniel, and a staghound named Darling, and Bella didn't know if it would make the situation better or worse if she pretended to find one of the animal pieces "quite interesting" instead of the one she'd accidentally chosen.

But before she'd had a chance to pivot to another piece—which would have been a difficult maneuver to attempt, anyway, given the size of this particular artwork—Lord Brooke had moved to stand beside her and was staring appreciatively at the canvas.

Bella decided to say nothing more, as it could only get her into further trouble. So she waited in silence, and finally Lord Brooke commented: "Somehow I don't think your mother would have approved."

A sudden vision of Lady Strickland's reaction to this image of young, barefooted women with their legs extending out from under their diaphanous frocks caused Bella to let out a gurgle of laughter. She quickly put a hand over her mouth to stifle the sound, but it was too late.

"I beg your pardon for laughing, but she thought it scandalous to even *pronounce* the word . . ." Bella felt foolish, but lowered her voice to a whisper before saying: ". . . 'leg'."

"I'm sorry, what did you say?" Lord Brooke asked.

Bella rolled her eyes at him. "You heard me."

He smiled. "I'm glad that you are not as easily scandalized as the late Lady Strickland. I am sure *she* would never call this painting 'quite interesting.'"

Bella stifled another giggle and quickly looked down at the catalogue in an attempt to regain her composure. "This is number fifteen, *Fairies*. And the painter is H. Howard."

Lord Brooke looked over her shoulder at the listing, and she could feel his breath tickling her neck. When he spoke, she couldn't suppress an involuntary shiver at the low voice so close to her ear. "It's based on a scene from Shakespeare's *Tempest*," he said, and proceeded to read aloud:

> *That on the sands with printless foot*
> *Do chase the ebbing Neptune, and do fly him*
> *When he comes back.*

"I have no idea what that means, but it sounds beautiful," Bella said, turning to look at him. She hoped he wouldn't think her ignorant, especially as she was sure Issie would have been able to quote the next line back to him, and Bella couldn't even recall what *The Tempest* was about. Apparently, barefooted fairies. But it didn't appear she'd disgusted him with her confession, as he was smiling warmly at her.

"It's not my favorite of Shakespeare's plays, but it seemed to prove inspiring to this artist," he said, turning his attention back to the painting. "Neptune is the god of the sea, and so Prospero is encouraging the fairies to chase the tide as it comes in and goes out."

Bella turned to study the painting as well, and now that she'd grown accustomed to the bare legs and décolletage, she did find that there was something enchanting about the artwork. The flowing dresses and draperies, and even the gracefully extended limbs, gave it a feeling of being in motion, as if the subjects were dancing in the moonlight.

But she was ready to move on to a different piece of art, and not the pet portraits, adorable as Darling indubitably was. "Which is your favorite painting of the collection?" she asked.

"I have not yet seen them all, but I am partial to Turner's latest," Lord Brooke said, offering Bella his arm and leading her to another, even larger painting.

It was difficult to wade through the dozens of people gathered around it, and Bella assumed this one was a favorite of many, not just Lord Brooke. She was not surprised, as she knew Turner to be extremely popular. Somehow Lord Brooke made a way for them through the crowd, though a few times Bella found herself holding on to his arm more tightly than was proper, and twice she was pushed against him almost as familiarly as she had been during their first encounter at St. James's Palace. She had the fleeting thought that if she was supposed to be protecting herself from becoming overfond of Lord Brooke, this was definitely not the way to go about it, as his proximity was having quite an effect on her.

But she quickly assuaged her conscience by reminding herself that this meeting had come about through no fault of her own while she was selflessly acceding to Issie's wishes, and so she was free to take whatever enjoyment she could from it.

Having made their way to the front of the crowd, Bella could now see the painting in its entirety, so she tried to ignore her reaction to Lord Brooke and turn her thoughts instead to assimilating what she saw.

The painting, *The Dort Packet-Boat from Rotterdam Be-*

calmed, stood out not only because of its size, as it was at least as tall as Bella was, but also because of the lightness and brightness of the work. "It's beautiful," she murmured, and then felt foolish at the inadequacy of that statement. Though she supposed it was a slightly more intelligent remark than the earlier one she'd made, that the *Fairies* painting was "quite interesting." It was a good thing she did not aspire to become an art critic. "The lighting . . . it's amazing," she said, trying again to express what made the painting such a joy to gaze upon.

Lord Brooke did not appear as if he had any fault to find with her conversation. "Yes, the lighting is remarkable. Especially in contrast to the darker works that surround it."

Bella forced herself to look away from the painting and saw that directly beside it there was another huge painting, this one of the Duke of Wellington on horseback wearing a black cloak, posed against a dark and gloomy sky. It was a very impressive piece as well but, as Lord Brooke had said, its darkness was a stark contrast to the bright, luminous riverscape Turner had painted. She turned her attention back to the Turner painting. "Did he inscribe his name, there?" she asked, pointing to a log floating in the river.

"He did. Ingenious, is it not?" They stood for another minute looking at the painting in silence, and then Bella turned to take a longer look at the painting of Wellington.

"My cousin and I used to think it was so romantic, the story of him and Kitty Pakenham. You know, how his father forced her to refuse him when they were young, but then he came back and married her over a decade later."

"You 'used to' think it romantic. You don't any longer?" he asked.

"Well, from the rumors I've heard it doesn't sound as if the marriage is a happy one."

"I'm no authority on the subject, of course, but I think it a grave mistake to marry because one feels honor bound to do so, and it seems as if obligation, rather than love, is what led him to marry her." They had both been looking at the painting as they spoke, but then Lord Brooke suddenly turned to look directly at Bella. "But that does not mean that the participants in a match contracted from duty cannot become sincerely attached to each other."

He was staring meaningfully at her, as if his words held some special significance, and she felt foolish that she did not grasp what he obviously intended her to. Perhaps it was some bit of family history that Issie would have known but that Bella was unfortunately ignorant of. Had Lord Brooke's sister made an arranged marriage that later became a love match? But before she could ask him for further explanation, she was jostled by someone trying to take a closer look at Turner's painting, and she realized that people were beginning to become annoyed at her and Lord Brooke.

He must have reached that conclusion at the same time she did, because he smiled at her and said: "We should perhaps give up our place to others not so fortunately situated," and led her away from the painting.

Though Bella dearly wanted to continue strolling through the gallery rooms with Lord Brooke as he showed her glorious works of art and read poetry in her ear (as there was more than one painting inspired by verse), she realized that Issie was probably looking for her, so she told him that she must return to her party.

"I will escort you. It really is not safe for you to flit about such a crowded place alone," he said, and looked around at the men surrounding them with such a fierce frown that many of them instinctively stepped back, even though Bella was sure they were just standing innocently nearby and had not the slightest intention of accosting her.

"I can see my cousin from here," Bella said, and hoped that was in actuality Issie's bonnet that she could just catch a glimpse of, "but I appreciate your concern, Lord Brooke. Thank you so much for showing me the Turner painting; it's spectacular."

And so saying, she walked quickly away from him and over to Issie's side. Thankfully, it *was* Issie, and after reaching her, Bella turned back to look at Lord Brooke. Seeing that he was standing where she'd left him and still looking in her direction, she gave him a smile and a nod, and he nodded in return. And then the crowds came between them and blocked him from view, and she had a sudden premonition of the future and the inevitable separation that was destined to come.

6

Issie *had* overtaxed her strength, and Bella was sorry she and the doctor had given in to her pleadings to visit the Royal Academy. The descent down the staircase had been harrowing for all of them. Until, that is, Dr. Jordan had come to Issie's rescue in a manner that would have been worthy of the hero of a romantic novel. They had made it little more than halfway and had paused at a landing as Issie was practically collapsing from fatigue, when the doctor suddenly picked her up and carried her the rest of the way down the spiral staircase.

Bella thought that there was no feat he could have performed that would have been more effective in awakening passionate adoration in a young woman's heart. Even Bella, who admired an entirely different gentleman, thought that if Issie wasn't already halfway in love with the doctor, she would have been tempted to fall in love with him herself.

Issie, who was exhausted, overstimulated, and dizzy from her descent down the circular stairs, stared at Dr. Jordan in dazed wonder on the carriage ride home, so that Bella, afraid Issie would embarrass both herself and the object of her adoration, finally suggested she sit back and close her eyes.

When they arrived at the townhouse, Dr. Jordan was prepared to carry Issie up the stairs, but the rest period in the carriage had revived her and she was able to make it to her bedchamber on her own two feet, though she leaned heavily on Dr. Jordan along the way. After she had been helped into bed he resumed his professional manner. "You should stay in bed tomorrow, Miss Grant," he said. "It is imperative that you rest." He then turned to address Bella. "Once she's recovered from today's exertions, have her walk the stairs again, twice per day. I will check back in a week." He then took his leave of them, but stopped in the doorway to address Issie once more. "Oh, and you should consume a beefsteak at least three times a week. You scarcely weigh a thing."

Before Issie could respond, Dr. Jordan was gone and the two cousins were left staring at each other in silence. "Bella," Issie said, in a hushed tone, as if she were in a dream and didn't want to talk too loud for fear of waking herself, "have you ever seen anything to match that?"

"Never," Bella replied softly but emphatically. "It was the most impressive thing I've ever witnessed."

"So then, it would be completely reasonable if I exerted all the strength I possess in trying to attach such a man."

"Completely reasonable. I will do everything in my power to assist you in such an endeavor. In fact, if you do not marry him, *I* might be forced to, just so such a specimen doesn't leave the family."

"You can't have him, Bella," Issie said, and Bella was sorry she'd joked about such a thing when she saw the anxious expression Issie now wore. She had no desire to undermine her cousin's already fragile self-confidence.

"I was teasing, love. He's all yours. That is very obvious."

"Maybe it is to you and to me, but I don't think it's obvious to him," Issie said.

"Perhaps not yet. But if you are diligent in following his prescription, he cannot help but be pleased with you. And didn't Shakespeare say: 'Some Cupid kills with arrows, some with traps'?"

Issie's eyes widened and she reached out to grab her cousin's hand. "Bella, did you just quote *Shakespeare*?"

"I don't know, did I?" Bella asked, not sure if she'd gotten the quotation, or the author, correct.

"Yes, you did. *Much Ado About Nothing,* Act 3." Issie smiled fondly at her cousin, her eyes a little watery. "This has been the best day of my entire life."

And Bella, thinking back to the incredible sights they'd seen, the time she'd spent with Lord Brooke in the gallery, and the joy she'd witnessed on her beloved cousin's face, felt it had been a rather wonderful day, as well.

Unfortunately for the cousins, Lady Dutton, who had benignly ignored them for the first few weeks of their visit, decided to stick an oar in.

While she and Bella were awaiting the day's callers, she told Bella that her cousin, the "poor relation," should do something to make herself useful. "If I didn't know better, I wouldn't even think she existed. I don't think I've seen her once since the day you both arrived in town."

Bella figured she should not contradict Lady Dutton by explaining she'd actually seen both of them many times, but that she couldn't tell Issie and Bella apart from each other. And Bella was definitely not going to tell her she was speaking to the "poor relation" at that very moment. "Her health is not good. As a matter of fact, I had to call for a doctor."

Lady Dutton harrumphed. "Blood always tells. There's a weakness there. Comes from the maternal line." Bella realized that Lady Dutton was referring to *her* mother, who was the daughter of an apothecary, since she believed that poor, lowly Arabella Grant was the sickly cousin. But Bella thought it was quite funny that the actual "Lady Isabelle" (who was, of course, the sickly one) *was* related to Lady Dutton through the maternal line. Bella and Isabelle were connected through their fathers, who were brothers, and so Bella was no blood relation of Lady Strickland or Lady Dutton, something for which she was extremely grateful. Especially when she heard Lady Dutton's next speech, which Lady Dutton thought she was directing to Isabelle. "Your mother was horrified Lord Strickland's brother married so far beneath him. I told her once that at least the child was legitimate, and she pointed out that was hardly a good thing, as if she hadn't been she could have been sent to the workhouse."

Bella had a very difficult time keeping her composure after this admission, as she was the child Lady Dutton had casually mentioned might have been sent to the workhouse which, for a three-year-old, was practically a death sentence. She had no doubt Lady Strickland would have sent her there regardless of her legitimacy, if Lord Strickland hadn't prevented her from doing that to his brother's child. But Lady Dutton hadn't finished with her tirade. "She has no business being sickly, anyway. Look at me, I'm nearly fifty"—she was at least sixty-five—"and don't coddle myself a bit. And that's my point: I shouldn't have to escort you all over town. She's too young to chaperone you to balls and the like, but it seems to me she can make herself useful and accompany you during the day."

"She has been doing so, as her health permits," Bella said, glad she had at least one example to support this statement. "We went to Somerset House yesterday to view the paintings of the Royal Academy, and we're going to Ackermann's tomorrow."

"Did Lord Brooke accompany you to Somerset House?"

"He did not escort us, but we met him there," Bella said, as she was aware Lady Dutton favored Lord Brooke's suit and would be horrified if she knew "Lady Isabelle" was limiting the time she spent in his company. And Bella, now that she'd become more familiar with London society, had come to realize what a prime catch Lord Brooke was. Of course Lady Dutton would be overjoyed to see him wooing the young lady she thought was her niece; every lady in town was desperate to capture his notice. However, he rarely paid court to eligible young women, which made his attentions to "Lady Isabelle" particularly noteworthy.

"It's too bad your mother didn't live to see this day, but it's gratifying that her plans for you are on their way to being achieved and that Lord Brooke is paying you serious attention. Just don't do anything to scare him away. I hope you've given up those bluestocking tendencies you used to have," she said, eyeing Bella suspiciously.

"Of course, Aunt. I hardly even open a book, these days."

"Wonderful," Lady Dutton replied.

Bella should have realized Lady Dutton was too experienced a campaigner to leave things to chance. When Lord Brooke called that day and asked "Lady Isabelle" to go riding with him on the next, the older woman intervened when Bella informed him she already had plans.

"Nonsense. It's merely an outing with her cousin," Lady Dutton said, and Bella jumped at the sound of her voice, as she hadn't realized Lady Dutton had been eavesdropping on their conversation. "They're going to some bookshop or another. You can escort them."

"Aunt, I'm sure Lord Brooke has better things to do—"

"Which shop? Hatchards?" he asked.

"Ackermann's," Bella told him, while trying to think of a way she could politely get out of it. She wished now that she had agreed to go riding with him. At least Issie wouldn't be present on such an excursion.

"I would be pleased to escort you and your cousin. It will finally give me an opportunity to make her acquaintance," Lord Brooke said, a genuine smile on his face. Bella could only muster up a fake one in response.

After the callers had left, she told Issie that she could not take her to Ackermann's the next day. "Bella, you promised!" Issie said, and Bella found it incredible how much her cousin had changed in these last few weeks. When they'd first arrived in town, she'd refused to accompany Bella anywhere, and now she was complaining that she had to stay at home. However, Issie had found her first and only London excursion so exhilarating that she was eager to repeat the experience. And since it was such a short, easy outing, Bella had initially encouraged her cousin to come with her.

"Lady Dutton insisted that Lord Brooke escort us, and I'm worried if you spend an entire afternoon with him in such close quarters he might figure out that *you* are Lady Isabelle. Though I'm probably being overly cautious. After all, it has been more than five years since he last met you."

"No, I probably shouldn't go," Issie said, her expression resigned. "That man is so exasperating."

"Issie," Bella protested, "it's hardly his fault that we are pulling an elaborate hoax on all of London society."

"I wouldn't put it quite like that, Bella. You make it sound unscrupulous, when in actuality it has had a number of quite positive effects, and may have literally saved my life."

"That's true at least. I can see that it's been extremely beneficial for your health."

"And don't forget how enjoyable it's been for you."

"I'm in no danger of forgetting *that*," Bella said sarcastically, as "enjoyable" was definitely not the word she would have used to describe her experience masquerading as her cousin. When she reflected on why it was not as enjoyable as it should have been, Bella began to feel slightly resentful that Issie could pursue *her* romance when she could not.

"I thought you didn't want to marry," Bella said a little irritably, startling Issie, who had begun reading when Bella had become preoccupied with her own thoughts.

"Well, I suppose I didn't, at first, but when he picked me up and *carried me down the stairs* . . ." Issie didn't finish her sentence, but sunk into her own reverie which, from the enraptured expression on her face, was a reliving of that moment at Somerset House.

"You changed your mind," Bella prompted her.

"What?" Issie asked, blinking. "Oh, yes. I changed my mind."

"And how do you propose to tell him who you really are? You don't think it will cause any problems when he finds out you've lied to him about your identity? That perhaps he will be upset with you when he discovers the truth?"

"Upset? When he finds out that I'm really Lady Isabelle and the possessor of a huge fortune? Hardly," Issie said, with a less-than-ladylike snort of derision. "I don't know how much money he has, of course, but I do not think he would have taken up a profession if he were wealthy, do you?"

"No," said Bella, discouraged to think Issie was most likely correct, and that Dr. Jordan would not be at all upset to discover her real identity. Unfortunately for Bella, the opposite was *not* true. It was perfectly fine from society's viewpoint to pretend to be someone of *lesser* wealth and prominence, but woe to the one who pretended the opposite.

"Besides, I mean to make him fall in love with me before I reveal the truth, and if he loves me, then he cannot possibly be upset with me," Issie said, and while Bella suspected love didn't necessarily work that way, she did wonder if Issie might not be onto something.

What if, instead of avoiding Lord Brooke, Bella accepted his invitations and spent as much time as possible with him? Then, if he chose to court her and their relationship did progress to the point where he desired to marry her, it would be a perfect test of his feelings when she revealed her true identity. Surely, if a man really and truly loved a woman, as Issie had pointed out, the prospect of never seeing her again would be entirely too painful, and he would be much more inclined to forgive her a small deception. Especially if she explained to him her very unselfish reasons for embarking on such a scheme in the first place.

The more time she spent in Lord Brooke's company, the more she realized he was nothing like Lady Strickland. He never made her feel inferior or demeaned her, but on the contrary, he always made her feel better about herself. And, while she'd have preferred to marry a man of lesser rank, she realized Lord Brooke wasn't to blame for his noble birth any more than she was for her lowly origins. She resolved, therefore, to attempt to win Lord Brooke's love, as Issie was doing with her doctor. If Issie could overcome her shyness and fight to win the man she wanted, surely Bella could do the same. Bella found her spirits lifting at the thought that she needn't suppress her desire to spend time with Lord Brooke, but could indulge herself as much as she wanted.

Issie, who had been a little disconcerted to find her usually even-tempered cousin in such an uncertain mood, was even more confused when Bella's frown cleared and she suddenly grabbed Issie's hands and began waltzing her around the room.

They were interrupted by a knock at the door, and Issie opened it to find Nancy there, holding a pile of linens.

"Beg pardon, mi—" she coughed as she addressed Issie so that whatever she'd said was unintelligible, "but Lady Dutton asked me to give you this mending to do."

Nancy held the pile out to Issie and she automatically took it, though she staggered a little under its weight. Bella rushed over to help Issie and Nancy quickly left, probably because she was afraid they'd try to hand the linens back to her.

"Aunt Lucretia is ridiculous!" Issie said furiously. "How dare she invite me to spend the season with her and then give me a bunch of old sheets to mend!"

"In her defense, she thinks she's giving them to me," Bella said dryly.

"That's not any better! She's as bad as my mother, treating you like a servant without even paying you a wage!"

"Your mother was worse; she made *me* pay *her*," Bella said, as she thought about how Lady Strickland appropriated her inheritance all of those years she'd lived with them.

"Bella, I hate to ask . . ." Issie said, looking at Bella with a pleading expression.

Bella sighed, as she realized what Issie was hinting at. But she also knew that Issie was a terrible seamstress, whereas she was very talented at needlework. And Bella didn't feel sewing was a very healthy pastime for Issie, anyway. She wanted her cousin spending her time out of doors, taking the air and getting exercise, not hunched over a bunch of fraying linens, repetitively wielding a needle back and forth. "I'll do it, Issie. I'm much faster than you."

"And you sew more even seams," Issie said, breathing a sigh of relief. "But don't do it too quickly, Bella, or she'll just find more for you to do."

Bella agreed to take her time over the task and went back to her chamber to do a little mending before she went out to "enjoy" her imposture as the Lady Isabelle.

Catherine had been happy to be invited on the Ackermann's excursion in Issie's place, though Lord Brooke looked very confused when he arrived to escort them. "Miss . . . Adams, is it not?" he said as he helped her into the coach. He had met Catherine a few times already that season and so was able to recall her name. He would never have become acquainted with her at all if the choice had been left to him, as he did not make a habit of consorting with social-climbing eighteen-year-olds, but he could not avoid meeting Miss Adams when she so persistently attached herself to Lady Belle's side.

Once they were all seated inside, Bella explained things to him. "My cousin feared having a relapse and so wasn't able to come, and since Miss Adams has been wanting to visit Ackermann's, I invited her instead."

"Well, I wouldn't say I had been *wanting* to visit, exactly, but Mrs. Mullins told me it would do me a world of good, especially when I told her *you* were going, Lord Brooke," Miss Adams said in her frank way, and Bella spared a sympathetic thought for Mrs. Mullins, who obviously had a more difficult task than Bella had at first realized. While Bella strongly believed a person should be truthful and was not happy about the fabrications she'd been guilty of since coming to town, there was something to be said for not blurting out *all* the truth, on every occasion, as Catherine Adams was prone to do.

Bella was very pleased with her first sight of Ackermann's, as it was a handsome shop with enormous windows at the front and a clerestory at roof level that admitted even more light into the sumptuously decorated rooms. And upon entering she was overwhelmed at the choices available to her. There were watercolors and rice paper, prints and framed art, illustrated books, writing desks and tea chests, et cetera, et cetera, et cetera.

Bella wasn't an admirer of Rowlandson, one of the artists Ackermann worked closely with; she found his caricatures ugly and vulgar and not at all funny, and she couldn't understand how or why there was a market for his work. But she did like the book *Microcosm of London,* which he had illustrated in collaboration with another artist, and enjoyed looking through it with Catherine. It felt to Bella as if she'd been able to take a tour of the entire city without having to travel anywhere. (And the book also included pictures of places ladies wouldn't have been allowed to visit anyway, like Brooks's gentlemen's club.) Bella thought about buying the book for Issie but then she saw an art book, *Six Progressive Lessons for Flower Painting,* and figured she could afford it *and* a box of watercolor cakes, which Issie might enjoy more.

She excitedly showed her purchases to Lord Brooke, who diligently admired them. "Do you paint?" he asked.

"No, unfortunately I'm a terrible artist. But my cousin is quite talented. These are for her."

"It's kind of you to buy her a gift, since she was unable to accompany us."

"Perhaps she can join us on another occasion," Bella said.

"I hope so, since I still have not had the pleasure of making her acquaintance. Though I do feel like I already know her, to some extent."

Bella's head shot up at this statement, and she fearfully asked, "Whatever do you mean?"

Lord Brooke looked surprised by her reaction. "Merely that you talk about her all the time, so much so that I've come to know a little about her habits and character. I didn't mean that I'd been secretively spying on her, so there's no reason for you to look at me so suspiciously," he said in a jocular tone, and Bella smiled in response.

Just then two women walked by and there were whispers of "Lady Belle" interspersed with giggling. Bella looked over at them, but didn't recognize either of the ladies, and she and Lord Brooke exchanged a glance. "Evidently, your popularity continues to grow," he said.

"I would be far happier if it did not. I do not understand what they find so amusing about me," Bella replied, bewildered. They had already greeted a number of people they both were acquainted with, as Lord Brooke was just as popular as Bella if not more so, but Bella had been surprised by the reaction she was receiving this afternoon. While people had spoken in a friendly fashion to Lord Brooke, they had practically smirked at Bella, and while none had laughed in her face, it seemed to Bella as if they'd wanted to. And while she was accustomed to being stared at and whispered about since becoming "Lady Belle," this reaction felt very different.

She hoped that her real identity hadn't been discovered, and that she was not about to be cast ignominiously from society.

Just then, Catherine, who had been perusing the latest caricatures, ran up to her side, breathless and big-eyed.

"Lady Belle, Lord Brooke, you must come immediately."

They obediently followed her to one of the walls of the shop, and she pointed to a caricature hanging just above eye level.

Bella was shocked to see a replica of her own face staring

back at her, with probably the same look of horror she was currently wearing.

It was a sketch of the scene from a few nights ago, at the ball where Mr. Peckham had lost his button in the middle of their dance. Bella, looking aghast at the situation she found herself in, was depicted standing across from Mr. Peckham's bent-over figure as he stooped to pick up his button. The artist, whoever he was, had drawn it from a vantage point *behind* Mr. Peckham, so that the first thing a viewer saw was his posterior, which had been enlarged and exaggerated, his tight breeches stretched across two ludicrously rounded orbs. Underneath the illustration appeared the caption:

"The Belle and the *Button*."

Bella, who usually did not appreciate such mean-spirited, vulgar, satirical prints, could not hold back a burst of laughter when she read the pun, and put a hand over her mouth a second too late.

Lord Brooke, who had been looking back and forth from the print to her face, appeared relieved at her reaction, and permitted himself a half smile.

Catherine was horrified. "Lady Belle! It is not funny! Indeed, it is not! This is all Mr. Peckham's fault. He should be held accountable." She turned suddenly to Lord Brooke. "Lord Brooke, perhaps *you—*" she began, and Bella quickly interrupted her, worried that the romantic young woman was going to suggest the men fight a duel over the silly incident.

"Catherine, you refine too much upon this," Bella said,

as soothingly as she could, as she was still trying to suppress her giggles. "This mean-spirited caricature is not the fault of Mr. Peckham. On the contrary, it was very rude of the artist to publish such an image of him." Bella's voice shook as she said this, as she was still struggling to keep from laughing, and her eyes had begun watering from her efforts to restrain her laughter. However, this made it appear to Catherine as if Bella were crying, and she suddenly grasped Bella to her bosom, hugging her tightly and rocking her.

"There, there, Lady Belle. How like you to expend your sympathy on someone who isn't worthy of it. You're too tenderhearted. He doesn't deserve your pity," Catherine said, and since she was built on more generous proportions than Bella—and Bella had already been holding her breath to avoid dissolving into giggles—Bella suddenly felt she was in serious danger of suffocation with her face pressed so tightly against Catherine's chest.

Thankfully, Lord Brooke intervened before Bella could make an even greater spectacle by swooning in a printshop in front of a caricature of herself. "Miss Adams, your loyalty toward Lady Belle does you great credit, but I think you can release her. We wouldn't want to cause even more of a scene."

Bella, after she'd had a chance to blink the moisture from her eyes and catch her breath, was alarmed to see he had reason for telling Catherine what he did. Every person in Ackermann's appeared to be watching them. However, when Bella looked at her audience, they all immediately turned their heads, chatting with great animation to the person standing next to them.

And while Lord Brooke did not volunteer to fight a duel in her honor, he redeemed himself in Catherine's eyes when he left Ackermann's the possessor of every copy of the scurrilous caricature.

After they dropped Catherine off at her home, Bella thanked him for what he had done. "It was very kind of you to try to protect my reputation in such a manner by purchasing those ridiculous prints, but I think this might be a case of shutting the stable door after the horse has bolted. Too many people have already seen it," she told him.

"I know. But it was a very small thing to do and it relieved some of my anger at the situation. I agree with your Miss Adams, you know. It was not the act of a gentleman for Peckham to expose you to ridicule as he did. But I think that he's been punished more than enough," he said, glancing at the stack of papers on the seat next to him.

"I agree. And at least the artist did not draw *me* in an unflattering manner, as he did poor Mr. Peckham." She reached out and took a paper from the stack, to look more closely at the depiction of her, which she had only glanced at earlier. Lord Brooke switched seats, ostensibly so they could look at the caricature together, though as soon as he sat next to her, Bella could not even comprehend what she was looking at, so disturbed was she by his nearness.

His shoulder brushed hers as he leaned forward and traced her sketched image with one finger. "It's not unflattering, but neither does it do you justice," he murmured, and Bella, for the second time that afternoon, felt she was in danger of suffocation. She reminded herself to breathe, even though the finger that had been tracing the picture suddenly reached up and tilted her face toward his, as if to compare her actual face with the drawing, and his eyes, which glinted in the dimly lit coach, began scanning her features as gently as his finger had traced her printed image.

"No, the original is far, *far* superior," he said, and she could feel a whisper of air as he finished the sentence, and her lips quivered from the faint breeze that brushed over them. Or perhaps they trembled because his lips were still removed from her own by an inch or two, and she desired him to come even nearer. However, he made no move to close the distance, and Bella finally, after what seemed like an interminable wait but was probably mere seconds, moved her own face forward. This appeared to be the permission he was waiting for, and he gently and tenderly touched her lips with his own.

Much too soon he drew away to look down into her face, smiling at her just as tenderly as he'd kissed her. "Bella," he whispered.

She returned his smile but was surprised when he suddenly moved back to the opposite bench, causing Bella to frown in confusion and feel forlorn and abandoned. But then she realized the coach had stopped without her even being aware of it and the door was beginning to open.

"I should have instructed the coachman to take a longer route after we dropped off Miss Adams," he said softly, blinking in the sudden light from the opening of the door.

And though she was still greatly disappointed at the interruption of her first kiss, she was pleased to see that Lord Brooke—who she very much doubted was as inexperienced as she was—looked as stunned and dazed as she felt.

He stepped out of the carriage and turned to help her, but instead of offering his hand he lifted her down by the waist, holding her there for a moment after her feet touched the ground. He released her with obvious reluctance, and she was just as reluctant for him to let her go, but she smiled tremulously at him before turning toward the Duttons' townhouse.

She didn't realize she was still holding a copy of the caricature until he reached for it. "Give that to me; I'll burn the lot of them as soon as I return home," he told her.

She held it beyond his reach. "No, I'd like to keep one," she said.

"Perhaps I will as well. Though I'll cut that idiot out of it."

"That should relieve your feelings and do far less damage than cutting his heart out in a duel," Bella said, laughing.

"Don't worry, he's safe from me. The person he should truly fear is Miss Adams," Lord Brooke said with a grin.

7

Bella ran up the stairs after saying goodbye to Lord Brooke, intent on reaching her room as quickly as possible so that she could have privacy in which to contemplate what had just happened between them. Unfortunately, Issie waylaid her before she could achieve her goal. And when Issie caught sight of the caricature Bella still held in her hand, Bella was forced to tell her what had happened at Ackermann's. (Though Bella decided not to mention the kiss that had occurred on the carriage ride home, since Issie disapproved of Lord Brooke so.) But the part of the story that upset Issie the most was when she discovered that Bella had taken Miss Adams in her place.

"Who is this girl, anyway? Who are her family?" Issie asked.

Bella looked at her cousin in shock. "Do you hear yourself, Issie? You sound just like your mother."

"I do not!" Issie exclaimed, horrified at the accusation, but then, thinking back to what she'd just said, had to acknowledge the truthfulness of Bella's remark. "Well, maybe I do, a little, but Mother would have asked those questions because she was pompous and arrogant, not out of concern and love for you, as I did."

"I appreciate your concern, but just because Miss Adams's family aren't blue bloods who came over during the Norman Conquest doesn't mean she has any nefarious purpose in befriending me."

Issie sniffed, and it was such a Lady Strickland mannerism that Bella gave her a significant look. "What?" Issie asked. "Why are you looking at me like that? My nose itched."

"Then I suggest you not raise it so high in the air," Bella replied. The two girls glared at each other, before Bella started laughing. "What are we even arguing about?"

"Miss Adams," Issie said, and though her expression had cleared, her tone made it obvious she was still feeling left out.

"If you had the chance to meet her you'd discover she's a very amiable, sincere young lady. In fact, I befriended her because she reminded me of you." Issie didn't look reassured by this statement, and Bella realized she was probably jealous of Catherine; perhaps even afraid the other young woman would replace Issie in Bella's affections. And since the cousins had been almost exclusively in each other's company from the time they were very young children, Bella could sympathize with her fears. Her tone softened and she said: "I will arrange for you to meet her very soon, Issie. We can walk in the park together one morning. Who knows, perhaps you and Miss Adams will become bosom friends and *I* will be the one feeling left out."

"I highly doubt it. You should be careful, Bella. She could be an opportunist taking advantage of your popularity to bask in the reflected glory."

Bella laughed at the idea of the very awkward and outspoken Miss Adams being a wily opportunist, and realized Issie would recognize how wrong she'd been as soon as she met her. In the meantime, there was no point arguing with her about it, so Bella turned to leave, hoping she could finally achieve a few minutes of privacy to daydream about Lord Brooke before she had to dress for the theatre. But she stopped in the doorway to turn back and say: "You needn't be concerned about her origins, at any rate. I've been told she's connected to the Adamses of Hampshire." She quickly shut the door behind her after making that announcement, congratulating herself that she'd had the last word.

Unfortunately, instead of taking an instant liking to each other, as Bella had hoped, the two ladies appeared to immediately *dis*like each other.

They met on an excursion to Hyde Park, and Bella had planned for it to occur early in the day to avoid most of the crowds. She thought this would have the advantage of making Issie feel more at ease, while also lessening their chances of running into as many of her own acquaintances. She did not want to be forced to introduce Issie to a lot of people, for both their sakes.

Issie reminded Bella that she could not call her by name while they were together. "Because, while it would not seem odd if I called you Belle or even Bella when your name is supposed to be Isabelle, it would seem very strange if you called me Issie when my name is supposed to be Arabella."

Bella agreed that such a thing would definitely provoke suspicion, even in a trusting person like Catherine, and so they finally decided Bella would avoid calling Issie anything at all. But, if absolutely forced to do so, she'd address her as "Cousin."

Bella wondered at the wisdom of what they were doing, but there were only a few weeks left in the season, and Issie's health had improved so much that Bella felt it would be unkind to keep her confined to her room. She also wanted Issie to have the opportunity of meeting other young people, as she'd been so sheltered in the past.

So Bella had decided upon this innocuous outing and was excited when she was able to persuade Issie to come. Although it didn't get off to a very auspicious start.

Both Miss Adams and Issie were inclined to be possessive of Bella, and as they'd each taken her by the opposite arm during their walk, Bella felt she was in danger of being torn in two. Particularly as Catherine, being taller and athletic, was inclined to walk at a much faster pace than the smaller, weaker Issie. Finally, Bella suggested they stop and sit on a nearby bench. "That way you and my cousin will have more of an opportunity to get acquainted," she explained to Catherine, who seemed disappointed that they'd come to walk in the park and were instead sitting as if they were in a drawing room.

Once they'd settled themselves on the bench, however, Issie hit upon the very topic Catherine would have preferred to avoid. "Exactly where in Hampshire are you from, Miss Adams?"

Catherine turned to Bella, panic-stricken, and Bella answered for her. "I never said Miss Adams was *from* Hampshire, just that she had family connections there."

"I beg your pardon," said Issie. "Where *do* you come from?"

Catherine continued to look petrified but managed to utter: "Derbyshire."

Bella decided she should intervene and direct the conversation away from Catherine's family background, before Issie began to wonder why Catherine looked so very self-conscious. "Miss Adams greatly enjoys sketching," she told Issie, before turning to Catherine and saying: "I believe I told you, Catherine, that my cousin is artistic as well."

But Catherine, terrified to say anything that would somehow reveal her lowly origins, merely nodded in reply, and there was an awkward and uncomfortable silence as Bella tried to think of something else the two young ladies had in common.

Unfortunately, one thing they did have in common, though they didn't yet know it, was walking toward them at that very moment.

Mr. Peckham, having caught sight of Bella, was eagerly

making his way to her side. He did not usually walk in the park so early, but he had recently had a new pair of trousers made and wanted to debut them to a small audience and gauge their reception before appearing in them at the more fashionable hour. They were in the Cossack style, which he had not previously favored as they seemed clownishly over-large to his eyes, accustomed as he was to wearing very tight breeches or pantaloons in the evening and equally tight trousers during the day. The Cossack trousers had been introduced to London society when Tsar Alexander and his entourage of Cossack soldiers had visited in 1814 for the peace celebrations, and they had been diligently copied by enterprising gentlemen directly afterward. But Mr. Peckham's tailor had convinced him that they were now, four years later, about to experience a resurgence in popularity, and that he was the man to lead that revival.

Therefore he now found himself in very high-waisted, striped trousers that puffed out at the hips, before gradually narrowing to his ankles, where they ended in straps that slipped under the soles of his feet. He felt self-conscious and extremely uncomfortable in such a great expanse of fabric. (Though it could be supposed that the roominess around his hips would have had the opposite effect.)

Bella, who was at her wit's end coping with Issie and Catherine, completely forgot about the caricature of a few days prior, and greeted him with a relieved smile. This was not at all the case with Catherine, who jumped up from the bench before he had even reached their side and said angrily, "You have some cheek, Mr. Peckham, to walk boldly over here like this!"

Mr. Peckham, who had no idea to what Miss Adams was referring, immediately assumed she was criticizing his trousers, and his cherubic face turned bright red and fell in dejection. At the same time he was struck by what an attractive picture the young woman made as she stood there confronting him, and he wondered why he had never noticed her before.

Catherine's generous, shapely figure was emphasized by the military-style walking dress and pelisse she wore, and its deep red color complimented her dark hair and eyes. In her anger she'd forgotten her usual shyness and awkwardness and was holding her head up high and proud and had her hands on her hips in a confident pose. It seemed to the embarrassed but admiring gentleman watching her that her eyes were practically emitting sparks, they shone so.

Issie, who had never met Mr. Peckham and at first did not know who he was, pieced it together after Miss Adams addressed him by name.

"Is he the one who lost his button?" Issie asked Bella in an aside that was quite audible to all present.

Miss Adams turned to her, their differences forgotten, and said, "You are correct, Miss Grant. This is the man who wronged your cousin."

Issie, who had at first not been overly concerned by the tale of the lost button, had grown angrier the longer she'd thought about it, as more was at stake than just Bella's public humiliation. It did neither of them any good to have such unflattering attention brought to Bella while she was masquerading as "Lady Isabelle." It also concerned her that there was now visual evidence of Bella's masquerade, though she had been relieved to learn that Lord Brooke had bought every copy. Still, Issie was almost as displeased with Mr. Peckham as Catherine was, and she rose from the bench to walk forward and lock arms with the other young lady standing belligerently before him, and treated him to her best imitation of her mother's frigid glare of disapproval.

Mr. Peckham, who was beginning to comprehend that it was not his trousers that were the problem, looked helplessly toward Bella. "Lady Belle, I do beg your pardon," he said, though he was unsure exactly what crime he was apologizing for. It had now been a week since the button incident had occurred and he had already apologized profusely for that, and he had no idea that there had been a caricature drawn and displayed afterward.

Nor did Bella wish him to find out about the caricature, because she knew he would be horribly crushed and humiliated. So it was her turn to glare, but she directed it at the two ladies who had so nobly risen to her defense. "Do not worry, Mr. Peckham. Miss Adams and Miss Grant are very fond of me and perhaps a little too eager to defend me from any perceived slights," she said, and though this still did not make the cause of the offense any clearer to Mr. Peckham, he was able to understand that at least Lady Belle was not angry with him.

But now the two young ladies who had been furious

with Mr. Peckham found that some of their annoyance was directed at Bella, since she should have been grateful to them for their loyal defense, instead of taking the side of the guilty party. So when Bella took Mr. Peckham's arm and resumed walking, the two young women, who had initially taken each other in dislike, now walked arm in arm behind the couple and, by means of grimaces, rolls of the eyes, and whispered complaints, found themselves in complete sympathy with each other.

Though she had achieved her goal of helping Issie make a new acquaintance, Bella wondered if she should have been more careful about setting such a goal. Because when she'd told Issie that she and Catherine might become bosom friends and that she'd be the one feeling left out, she hadn't realized she was such a gifted prophet.

However, after dismissing Mr. Peckham and squeezing herself into her former spot beside the two ladies, she had soon worked herself back into their good graces, and they were laughing and chatting happily when they heard themselves being addressed.

"Lady Belle, Miss Adams," a masculine voice called, and Bella's heart began beating at an accelerated rate even before she saw Lord Brooke's face.

The ladies had been so engrossed in their own conversation they had not seen him approaching, and so Bella had no option but to introduce him to Issie.

She and Issie had discussed it before venturing out

together again in public, and they had concluded that Lord Brooke had only met Issie once, more than five years ago. Surely, he wouldn't recognize her all these years later. She was now a mature young woman, not a child, and the exercise and diet regime had changed her appearance even further. So, while Issie would never have sought him out, and neither did she want to spend lengthy periods of time in his company, she and Bella were no longer panic-stricken by the fear that were he to meet Issie again he would immediately guess their secret. Though they couldn't help feeling a trifle nervous now that the moment had arrived.

But it did not appear that he had any suspicions at all. He reacted very courteously to the introduction, bowing over Issie's hand and telling her how pleased he was to meet her. "Your cousin speaks of you quite often," he said with a warm smile, "and I was disappointed I have not had the opportunity to meet you before now."

Issie did not say much, merely nodding and offering a slight smile in return, but Bella was relieved that there was nothing in Issie's behavior to give away the fact that she'd already met Lord Brooke and had taken him in dislike.

There was also the distraction of Catherine's presence, which Bella did not know whether to be grateful for or not. Miss Adams did not appear at all shy with Lord Brooke, and somehow when they resumed their walk *she* was the one who ended up on his arm, with Bella trailing behind them with Issie. As they walked, Catherine enthusiastically told Lord Brooke about how they'd seen Mr. Peckham earlier and she'd been able to give him a resounding set-down.

The ladies had been on their way out of the park when they'd encountered Lord Brooke, so after Catherine told her story he took his leave of them. Bella reflected that, now that she'd decided to try to make Lord Brooke fall in love with her before revealing her true identity, she seemed to be continually thwarted in this endeavor. Or at least, she'd been prevented from spending time with him without Catherine Adams being present, as well.

But before leaving, Lord Brooke turned to address Bella directly. "Lady Belle, I spoke to your great-aunt and she agreed that we could go riding together tomorrow. I will arrange for a mount and see you at eleven. Until then," he said, with a smile for her and her alone.

"I look forward to it," Bella replied, repenting of the slight resentment she'd felt toward Catherine for monopolizing Lord Brooke. However, when he was walking away (but still appeared to be within hearing distance), Catherine said in her usual, overly loud speaking voice: "Mrs. Mullins calls Lord Brooke 'The Uncatchable Catch,' but I think you may have caught him, Lady Belle." And Bella felt that, this once, she may have been a little too quick to grant forgiveness.

Bella was thrilled to be on the back of a horse again; it had been much too long since her rides in the country, and while Rotten Row in Hyde Park could not compare to her rambles around Fenborough Hall, it was still very pleasant to feel the spring breeze rustle her hair and the bay mare she rode respond to her slightest command. But what made it most exciting of all was the presence of Lord Brooke, who was the picture of health and vigor astride his black Arabian stallion, and who frequently looked over at her with a smile that seemed to imply he was as delighted by her presence as she was by his.

The Serpentine, its waters sparkling in the late morning sunlight, ran parallel to their riding path, and they eventually dismounted to walk alongside it. They did so in companionable silence for a few moments, before Lord Brooke said: "I was pleased to finally have the opportunity to meet your cousin, and to find that she does not appear as sickly as I'd imagined her to be. I hope that her health is improving?"

"It is. She has improved tremendously since we've come to town. She has a new physician, a Dr. Jordan, who is absolutely marvelous," Bella said enthusiastically.

"An older, fatherly type, this Dr. Jordan?" Lord Brooke asked.

"On the contrary. He's probably your age, if not a year or two younger. And surprisingly handsome."

"*Surprisingly* handsome? That's an interesting turn of phrase."

"His appearance surprised my cousin, at any rate," Bella said, giggling. "She's had no familiarity with young, handsome doctors. Or handsome men in general."

"I see. Perhaps that explains her rapid improvement," Lord Brooke suggested.

"I definitely think it had something to do with it," Bella

agreed. "Somehow she's more responsive to his admonishments that she exercise and eat regularly than she's ever been to mine." Bella said this in a self-mocking tone and Lord Brooke smiled in response.

"You told me before that she came to live with you as a young child. Does she have any money of her own, or is she fully dependent on you and your family?" he asked.

Bella reminded herself that she had to be on guard, because it would be easy for her to make a slip now that he was asking questions about her own background, yet she had to reply to him as if she were Issie. "She has a small competence, but not enough to set up an establishment of her own," Bella said, though it felt strange to be speaking of herself in the third person. Still, this was a good opportunity to discover how Lord Brooke viewed impecunious young women of absolutely no consequence. "She was three when she came to live at Fenborough Hall."

"And if your mother wasn't particularly motherly to you, she probably showed even less affection to a poor relation," Lord Brooke said sympathetically.

"You're right; my cousin was not treated kindly at all. The family did not approve of her parents' marriage, you see." Bella then proceeded to outline her own family background while telling the story as if she were Lady Isabelle. She explained to Lord Brooke that Lord Strickland's younger brother had been expected to marry an heiress from a neighboring estate, so when he broke it off it caused a major scandal. And it was made even worse when he eloped with the daughter of a village apothecary. Bella paused to look up into Lord Brooke's face and gauge his reaction to this shocking misalliance. However, if he disapproved, his expression and voice gave no indication of it.

"He sounds like a very courageous man, to go against the wishes of his family, and society as a whole. As a younger son he probably had even more reason to make an advantageous marriage, so to marry an impoverished young woman was a very unselfish act."

"*I've* always thought so," Bella said. "Of course, Lady Strickland, my mother, did not agree."

"No, I can very easily imagine what her reaction would be," Lord Brooke said dryly.

"I found out recently that she wanted to send . . . my cousin to the workhouse after her parents died." Bella had to remind herself again halfway through this speech that she was supposed to be Issie. She was still so angry and upset at what Lady Dutton had told her that it had nearly caused her to forget her role.

"That's unconscionable!" Lord Brooke said angrily. "Send a three-year-old, her own niece, to the workhouse? I beg your pardon, I know she was your mother, but I found her a difficult woman to like on the few occasions we met, and this just confirms my poor opinion of her."

"You needn't beg my pardon. I was not at all fond of her. She made my life miserable," Bella said, and no longer knew if she was speaking as Issie or herself. Both, she supposed. Issie would have agreed with everything Bella had said about Lady Strickland, even though she *was* her mother.

"I am so sorry," Lord Brooke said, stopping and turning to look at her. "You didn't deserve such treatment."

"No one deserves such treatment," Bella said.

"You are right, of course, but it particularly pains me to think of *you* being treated in such a way. You're so bright, and lovely, and . . . so very sweet," he said, his voice lowering. He reached for her hand, and though she wore kid gloves, he pushed up the lace ruffle of her sleeve to expose her wrist and, raising her hand, pressed a kiss on the bare flesh he'd uncovered. Bella shivered in response to the featherlight caress, but then she heard an approaching horse and rider and quickly pulled her hand away.

The horseman was known to Lord Brooke and they greeted each other, but Bella was relieved when he didn't stop to talk, as it would have interrupted her conversation with Lord Brooke and she might not have been able to find a way to return to the topic of her "cousin's" parentage. She realized that, while Lord Brooke seemed to be sympathetic to what she'd described of her real situation, she still was not sure if he would ever contemplate making a marriage like her father had; one based on love, and not family connections or obligations. And this was the perfect opportunity for her to find out.

So she took a deep breath, gathered her courage, and asked: "Would you ever consider making such an unequal match, like my uncle did? Marrying someone poor, and from a lower class of society?"

He looked surprised by the question and shot her a piercing look. "I haven't had to consider it," he finally said, "as

I've not met someone in that situation who ever tempted me into marriage."

This was not a very satisfactory answer, in Bella's view. "But if you did . . ." she prompted.

"Are you asking this for curiosity's sake, or because you are seeking advice for yourself?" he asked.

"Why would I be seeking advice for myself?" Bella asked, confused.

"I am not sure. Perhaps you have met someone from a lower class of society, maybe from the professional classes, and are considering following your uncle's example."

It took Bella a moment before she realized he was referring to Dr. Jordan. He obviously had misconstrued her praise of the man and was now imagining she was contemplating an alliance with a socially obscure doctor. Which the real Lady Isabelle *was* contemplating. It was all too comical, and Bella laughed. And when she did, Lord Brooke's serious expression lightened.

"Have I misinterpreted matters?" he asked hopefully.

"Entirely. I am not contemplating such a match," Bella said. "I was asking merely for curiosity's sake, and to gain a better understanding of *your* character."

"That *is* a relief. Because, while I am not at all jealous of Mr. Peckham, competing for your affections against a 'marvelous, surprisingly handsome' physician, not to mention one who rescued your beloved cousin from the brink of death, seems like a task beyond my abilities."

"I think you underrate yourself," Bella said, with a flirtatious look, and he laughed in response.

"Perhaps I do. Would you like to enumerate my good qualities, so that I will be encouraged to continue in my courtship?" Lord Brooke asked.

"Oh, no," Bella said with a saucy smile. "I would not like to encourage you so much that you cease to make an effort."

"Believe me, my lady, courting you is not an effort. It's a pleasure."

Bella looked up and their eyes met, and the words he spoke and the tone he spoke them in, combined with the warm glance he bestowed upon her, caused a curious tightening of her stomach.

And then he returned to their previous subject. "While it's true, as I mentioned earlier, that I've never been tempted to court a woman from a lower class of society, I've also never believed bloodlines, rank, or social status are indicative of a person's true worth. It is a source of wonder to me that Lady Strickland's narrow-minded prejudices did not negatively affect you, and that you are so openhearted and accepting of others," he said, his gaze so warm and admiring that she could almost imagine he *was* touching her. But at the same time she very much knew he was not, and she felt a pang at the knowledge he could not take her into his arms, there in the middle of Hyde Park.

"*You* are a wonder to me, Bella," he said huskily. "Whoever first called you that was very wise, as you are not only exceedingly lovely of face and form, but beautiful at heart."

And then, just when she thought he would take her in his arms regardless of their surroundings, they were hailed once again by an acquaintance and the opportunity was lost.

Upon returning to the Duttons' townhome after her ride with Lord Brooke, Bella was dismayed to run into Lord Dutton, whom she hadn't seen since their encounter in the breakfast parlor weeks earlier.

They met in the hall, outside the drawing room, and Bella bobbed a slight curtsy with a murmured, "Good afternoon, my lord."

"Good afternoon," he replied. "May I speak with you a moment?"

She nodded and he turned to walk into the drawing room, passing the footman who was stationed at the door. She followed, and after she'd entered the room he closed the door.

"I will not keep you long. I merely wanted to inform you, outside of the servants' hearing, that you need not be in fear of meeting me. I will not give away your and Lady Isabelle's secret."

Bella was embarrassed that this very distinguished gentleman was aware of their deception. "I am so sorry, my lord. What must you think of us, deceiving your wife, and the rest of society, in such a way?"

"As far as Lady Dutton is concerned, she began this by deceiving herself, so you need feel no guilt on her behalf," Lord Dutton replied.

"I don't understand."

"It's true her eyesight is not good; she needs spectacles and vanity prevents her from wearing them, but she also chose to believe what she wanted to believe. When presented with you and your cousin, I am sure she could not bear to accept that the sicklier, less attractive, socially awkward Lady Isabelle was related to her, and that *you* were the despised product of a misalliance. If you and your cousin had not exploited her assumption for your own reasons she would have eventually been forced to accept Isabelle as her niece, but when you did not correct her she obviously concluded her instincts had been proven correct. However, I think if you hadn't begun your little masquerade the consequences would have been far worse. She would have been constantly disappointed in Isabelle and made sure she was aware of it, and your cousin's stay in London would have been miserable, to say the very least."

"Thank you for explaining this to me, my lord. It does relieve my mind of some of the guilt I've felt at the deception we've been engaging in. Issie has had to live with disapproval and disdain her entire life and it would have been distressing to both of us if she'd had to endure more of that these past two months," Bella said.

"Yes, well, you needn't explain yourself to me, but I did want you to know that I have no plans to expose your secret. In fact, I am curious to see how long you can successfully dupe London society." Lord Dutton permitted a slight smile to cross his unexpressive, aristocratic face.

"I hope we're successful for the last three weeks of the season, at least," Bella said, with a grimace.

8

Dr. Jordan was scheduled to return and appraise Issie's progress the next afternoon, so Bella refused an invitation to drive in Hyde Park with Lord Brooke, and took a great deal of pleasure in explaining to him the reason why. But as she was supposed to see him that evening at dinner, he was not too disappointed to learn that she was spending the afternoon with Dr. Marvelous.

Issie had improved so much that it seemed unnecessary for the doctor to come to her bedchamber; she was no longer so weak she needed to lie in bed for her examination and was perfectly capable of meeting him in the drawing room. However, she was hesitant to do so.

"What if Aunt Lucretia comes in while he's there?" Issie asked, and Bella acknowledged that such a scenario would not be pleasant. It wasn't that they still feared Lady Dutton would discover their true identities, but rather that if Issie met with the doctor in Aunt Lucretia's presence she would make things exceedingly awkward, and might berate Issie for calling in a doctor at all.

Therefore, Issie and Bella decided to have him come up to Issie's room, as he had for past visits. Issie was wearing another of her new dresses (salvaged from Bella's closet before she'd altered it), this one a dusky rose color, and Bella had applied a little rouge to her cheeks and lips, even though she hardly needed it, as her color had improved a great deal and she no longer appeared deathly pale. In fact, Bella later wondered if instead of rouge they should have applied rice powder.

Because, instead of smiling at the sight that greeted him when he entered—and Issie was such a fresh, pretty sight her appearance would have brought delight to just about anyone—Dr. Jordan scowled at her.

"Why are you in bed?" he asked.

"Well, I—because I knew you were coming," Issie stuttered, her expectant smile fading.

"I hope that I didn't give you the impression I wanted you to wait for me in bed," the doctor said, and then turned bright red, as if it suddenly occurred to him how horribly his words could be misconstrued.

Bella turned a smothered laugh into a cough, and since Issie merely looked confused, she decided she had better intervene. "We apologize, Doctor. We were unsure where you would prefer to examine my cousin, which is the reason she's in bed in the middle of the afternoon. But she has been following your prescription to the letter and does not take to her bed during daylight hours any longer. She's been very diligent, and I think you will be very pleased with her progress."

The doctor, his color still heightened, nodded and murmured, "Yes, she is looking very well. Almost *too* well." Both Bella and Issie hoped he wasn't referring to the rouge when he made that remark. "Have you been experiencing any more heart palpitations?"

"Not very often," Issie answered a little hesitantly, and Bella wondered if perhaps she was having them at that very moment. Especially as the doctor drew closer to her bedside and, as he had on his first visit, leaned down to put his head against her chest and listen to her heart.

"Please cough," he said.

And Issie, who had tightly shut her eyes, obediently gave a little cough. She still had her eyes closed when Dr. Jordan removed his head from her chest.

"You needn't close your eyes," he told her. But when Issie opened them the doctor's face was still uncomfortably close to her own, and Bella thought she probably wanted to shut them again.

"Have you been experiencing any more weakness or trembling in your extremities?" he asked.

"No," said Issie, in an uncertain tone that seemed to contradict her denial. Especially when she clasped her hands together as if to still their trembling.

The doctor stepped a few feet away and turned to address Bella. "She's been taking regular exercise?"

"She walks the stairs at least twice a day, and we've also

gone on other outings. We went for a walk in Hyde Park two days ago."

"And you've been eating beefsteak?" he asked, turning to look at Issie again.

She wrinkled her nose in distaste. "Since you insisted, yes. I am not very fond of it, however."

"I am sorry you dislike the taste, but it's been just a little over a week and I can already see an improvement," the doctor said, his glance darting over Issie's figure in a professional appraisal. If he admired what he saw, his expression did not reveal it. His eyes returned to her face and he gave a quick nod. "Well, Miss Grant, while it's too early to say if you are fully recovered, and your heart rate is still slightly more accelerated than I could wish, you have made a most remarkable improvement since I first visited you. I am very pleased with your progress."

He smiled at Issie at the conclusion of this speech, and she returned his smile, happy to receive even such mild praise for her efforts. But at his next words her smile disappeared. Turning to include Bella in his remarks, he said: "It has been a pleasure meeting both of you ladies. I hope you enjoy the rest of your stay in town."

"What do you mean?" Issie asked, her voice rising. "Surely you will visit me again?"

He shook his head. "There is no need. If you continue on your current regimen you will soon be fitter than the majority of ladies in London. Unless, that is, you are experiencing some other symptoms that you neglected to tell me about."

"Well—" Issie began, but Bella shook her head at her behind the doctor's back. She did not want Issie inventing illnesses in order to see Dr. Jordan again.

"What my cousin is trying to say, Doctor, is that, while she may not need to see you again in a *professional* capacity, we enjoyed our time with you at the Royal Academy and would be pleased if you would accept another invitation. Perhaps to the theatre to see one of the plays you and my cousin are so fond of quoting. Or you and Miss Grant could finally visit Ackermann's, as you had initially planned."

Dr. Jordan looked slightly unsure, but then turned to look at Issie. "Is that something you would enjoy, Miss Grant?"

"More than anything," she said, her heart in her eyes.

"Then I would be very pleased to accompany you," he said. And he smiled at Issie in a manner that did not seem strictly professional.

Bella and Lady Dutton had been invited to a private dinner that evening at the house of a society matron, Lady Amelia Clayton, who had launched her own daughter that season. Bella was surprised that she had been invited, as she was not at all friendly with Miss Clayton. (Although it was actually Miss Clayton who had turned up her snub nose at Bella, because Bella was willing to be friends with just about anyone.) The mystery of her invitation was solved when Sir Roger told Bella that Lady Amelia had gotten the other gentlemen to attend by promising that Lady Belle would be there.

At first, Bella had reason to be thankful for her false identity, because if she'd been attending as lowly Miss Grant, she would have been seated below the salt with the other hangers-on and the octogenarian who kept falling asleep over his dinner. After her experience of having a relative suddenly drop dead, Bella was concerned a few times that *this* gentleman was not merely napping, but taking his eternal rest, and was relieved when Mr. Peckham, who was seated not too far from him, poked him and woke him up.

Because of her high rank as "Lady Isabelle," she'd been seated next to Lord Brooke, who would have been the dinner partner she'd have chosen if given the choice. However, the dinner still seemed excruciatingly long, as she was forced to converse at least half the time with the gentleman on her other side, who was the husband of Lady Amelia and the host of that evening's gathering. He insisted on describing a fox hunt he'd held at his country estate in exhaustive detail, complete with every person who was on the guest list (many of whom Bella did not know), what was served for dinner each evening, and an incomprehensible explanation of the chase the fox had led them on.

She was finally freed from the table to retire to the drawing room, and after a short time spent alone with the other ladies—who reminded Bella of cats prowling for the best spot from which to leap upon their quarry—the gentlemen rejoined them.

Lord Brooke was the juiciest prey and was quite literally pawed by a few ladies as he made his way into the room, but he was eventually able to extricate himself and reach

Bella's side. Unfortunately, a few of the other gentlemen had the same goal he did, so he wasn't able to have her all to himself.

The group surrounding Bella was talking of nothing in particular and laughing at the same, when their conversation was abruptly interrupted by Lady Dutton announcing that Lady Isabelle should play for them.

"For she has had the best instructors and is quite 'professhent,'" Lady Dutton said. (Bella thought she must have confused the words "professional" and "proficient" and was glad Issie wasn't there to be mortified by her aunt's mistake.)

"We would be happy to have Lady Isabelle perform for us," Lady Amelia said. And she said this very sincerely, because if Lady Belle were playing the pianoforte, the gentlemen would be forced to leave her side and perhaps pay attention to another of the young ladies present, such as her daughter.

"I beg your pardon, Aunt, but you are mistaken. I do not play at all well, and do not wish to subject those present to my poor efforts," Bella said with a smile that appeared carefree to those watching but covered a very real fear that she was about to be unmasked.

It was true that Issie had had the best of instructors and was very skilled at playing the pianoforte, but Bella was not. Bella's aunt had not permitted her to pursue the accomplishments of a genteel young lady, such as sketching, or watercolors, or learning to play the pianoforte or harp. If anyone deigned to marry Bella, which Lady Strickland didn't think at all likely, it would probably be a country vicar or a member of the professional classes, who couldn't afford a wife with expensive hobbies. So she had been encouraged to pursue her talent at sewing and had even been taught to cook, as her aunt thought those were the extent of the skills Bella would need in the bleak future Lady Strickland had envisioned for her.

Bella had snuck into the music room on occasion and Issie had taught her a few simple tunes, and Bella had also sung while Issie accompanied her; but she had never performed in front of an audience and felt she would merely embarrass herself if she did so now. And it would become very clear to everyone if she attempted the few simple songs she'd learned that she was neither a professional nor at all proficient.

But Lady Dutton was not going to accept Bella's refusal without argument. "Nonsense, Isabelle. There's no need for false modesty," she said sternly.

And then Lord Brooke spoke up. "It has been many years since I last heard you play, Lady Belle, but I remember being quite impressed. Especially as you were only fourteen at the time."

Bella had not realized that Issie had performed for him when she'd visited Bluffton Castle, but she could very well imagine Lady Strickland insisting that Issie do so. It was the one thing about Issie that she had taken pride in.

"I am very sorry," Bella said, her smile no longer in evidence, "but I do not wish to perform this evening."

There was a pall cast over the gathering at Bella's refusal, and she lowered her head in embarrassment. But then the taciturn Sir Roger unexpectedly came to her rescue. "I haven't got an ear for music, myself," he said, breaking the awkward silence. "If we're going to play something, how about cards?" Since there were other avid card players in the group, his suggestion was taken up with enthusiasm and a few tables were formed.

While this was happening, Lord Brooke leaned closer to Bella and quietly apologized. "I'm sorry, I should have realized you didn't want to play. I thought you just needed encouragement to do so."

"It is perfectly all right," Bella answered, but her expression gave the lie to her remark. Lord Brooke had very rarely seen her when she wasn't in a cheerful mood, and he realized that for some reason she was highly disturbed. He thought it strange that she was able to brush off the far more embarrassing incident with the button and its resulting caricature with a smile, even laughter, but that a request to play the pianoforte had caused her such distress. He wondered if she associated such a command with her mother and it brought back painful memories.

He realized she must have been more scarred by her childhood than he had previously thought. She had been very successful at hiding her hurt behind her playful, lively manner, but at this moment, when the mask slipped, he discovered she was far more complex than the vivacious "Lady Belle" she presented to the world. He felt a protective tenderness sweep over him, a desire to shield her from further hurt. But more than anything else he wished that she would lower the guard she'd put up around her. He was aware that she had been holding him at arm's length the first few weeks of the season, and he thought he had understood why; he had been unsure, as well, if *he* wanted the commitment that a serious courtship inevitably resulted in. He also didn't like the idea of fulfilling their mothers' wishes for them, even though both women were dead and gone. His greatest fear was that she would reject him for a similar reason; that she would marry someone like that handsome doctor, in a belated and futile attempt to rebel against the expectations her mother had had for her.

The tea tray arrived and she asked him if he'd like a cup, and he was relieved that she was looking a little less woebegone, though he did see a tinge of apprehension in her gaze when she met his eyes, and he hoped he wasn't the one who had caused it.

"Why don't I get *you* a cup," he suggested, and her lovely smile made a brief reappearance. Lord Brooke was actually relieved when Mr. Peckham stepped forward to take his seat after he left to walk over to the tea tray, as he did not consider Peckham a serious rival for Bella's affections, and thought his jovial, undemanding company was likely just what she needed.

As long as the idiot didn't drop anything on her, like the contents of the sloshing cup of hot tea he was presently holding.

Bella was sure that Lord Brooke must be suspicious of her after her refusal to play for the company that evening, but on the way home she found that it was Lady Dutton who demanded an explanation.

"I do not understand. Why did you claim that you were not able to play? I have heard you practicing since you came to town. And your mother told me you were well trained."

"That was my cousin you heard playing," Bella said.

"Where did she learn to play so well? Surely, your mother didn't pay for *her* to have lessons?"

"Of course she didn't," Bella said, irritated by the way Lady Dutton said the word "her," as if even making a reference to Bella caused a bad taste in her mouth. "Lady Strickland—my mother—would have never wasted a penny on the lowly child she so despised."

"Well? How did she learn, then?" Lady Dutton asked, not at all conscious of the sarcasm in Bella's remark.

Bella sighed. "She must be naturally talented, I suppose," she said, turning to gaze unseeingly out at the gaslit streets and saying very little for the rest of the short journey.

It was long past midnight when they returned home, and normally Bella would not have thought of waking Issie so late, but she was too upset to exercise such consideration. That moment when the entire party had turned to look at her and she'd had to admit that she could not play the pianoforte had been far more humiliating than Mr. Peckham's ridiculous behavior during their dance or that silly caricature. She had been so sure that she was on the verge of being branded a liar and a cheat in front of Lord Brooke and

her other gentlemen friends, the few people whom she'd
met whose opinion mattered to her.

What excuse could she give, what explanation could she
offer, if she was suddenly and publicly exposed? At least if
she went to Lord Brooke and confessed the truth he would
be more inclined to listen to her explanation of the reasons
she'd tricked him.

And even if her fear of discovery was exaggerated, she
still found the experience humiliating, as it plainly illustrated that she did not fit in with those of Lord Brooke's
class. She had not been trained in the accomplishments considered essential for a young lady of quality. She was a fraud
in more ways than one. Her very real feelings of inferiority,
feelings she'd fought her entire life, threatened to over-
whelm her. She felt as common and ill-bred as her aunt had
always told her she was.

So she went upstairs and into Issie's bedchamber, carrying a lighted candle to her cousin's bedside, before gently
shaking her by the shoulder when the light alone failed to
wake her.

"Issie, wake up."

It took a few minutes before Issie was finally sitting up
in bed and coherent enough to ask: "What is the matter?
Why did you wake me?"

"I think we should end this, Issie. I want to tell Lord
Brooke the truth and stop pretending to be you."

"What?" Issie asked, shaking her head a little, as if to
clear it. "I don't understand. Why now? The visit is almost

at an end; we have less than three weeks left! You can't confess *now*, Bella. If you told Lord Brooke, you'd have to tell Lady Dutton as well; it would be a complete disaster. And it makes no sense; we had planned to just go home at the end of the season without anyone having ever been the wiser. Why confess to something when we do not have to?"

"Because I was almost exposed this evening," Bella said, and explained what had happened that had so alarmed her.

"You are making far too much of it. Yes, if this had happened at the very start of our visit, there would be reason for your fears. But we've been here for two months. Everyone, including Lord Brooke and Lady Dutton, has accepted you as Lady Isabelle, even after meeting me. They are not going to suddenly become suspicious at this late date."

Bella knew that everything Issie had said was true, but she did not feel like being rational, she was so very tired of it all. She wanted to meet Lord Brooke with nothing between them, to know, beyond any doubt, that he wanted to court *her*, not Issie. She wanted to be able to have a conversation with him without having to carefully consider each word before she said it. She wanted him to fall in love with Arabella Grant, not Lady Isabelle.

She was also tired of the endless balls and entertainments when she heard herself announced as "Lady Isabelle" and saw all heads turn her way. Popularity and adulation meant less than nothing when you weren't sure why you were receiving it and you didn't believe yourself deserving of it.

But she supposed Issie was correct and that it would be foolish, even disastrous, not to keep their secret a mere two and a half weeks longer.

"Besides," Issie continued, "I am not ready to tell Dr. Jordan the truth. He is taking me to Lackington's Temple of the Muses bookshop tomorrow and has promised to show me other London sights, and I don't want to do anything to scare him away. He says Ackermann's is where the idle rich go to see and be seen, but that Lackington's has the most books for the best value, and he wants to purchase a new series of engravings of the human skeleton. Do you think he'd be offended if I offered to pay for it?"

Bella thought that he probably would, based on his comment about the "idle rich." She also wondered if Issie would have a more difficult time of it than she'd imagined when it came to confessing her true identity to the doctor. Overcome by dejection all of a sudden, Bella let out a heavy sigh and Issie eyed her in concern.

"Bella," Issie said, reaching out to grasp her cousin's hand, her expression serious, "I do apologize. I know that you did not want to embark on this deception from the first, and that I've taken advantage of your good nature. I don't know why I'm so weak and you're so strong; especially since my mother treated you just as badly as she did me, if not more so. Maybe you inherited courage from your parents. Lord knows they would have needed it to defy our family like they did." Bella was alarmed to see tears well up in Issie's eyes. "But I think my mother *broke* something in me, Bella. I really don't think I could have gone out into society, feeling as I do about myself."

"Issie, you can't believe the things she told you!" Bella said, though one part of her brain recognized the irony of telling Issie not to do something she'd just been doing herself. "She's dead now, and may God forgive me for saying this, but I'm glad she's gone. Everything she told you was cruel and—and totally *wrong*! You are *so* intelligent and pretty and talented. It's one of the reasons I hate pretending to be you; because I don't possess half of the talents that you do. Believe *me,* Issie, not her. Would I love you so much if you weren't wonderful?"

Now both girls had tears running down their faces, and Issie sniffed, but in a skeptical manner. "I think you decided to love me when you were three, and nothing I did could ever change your mind."

"I was very precocious and a great judge of character," Bella said, grinning through her tears, before she sat down on the bed next to Issie and hugged her. "It's all right, Issie. I will see this pretense out till the end. But I want you to promise me that you will try your best not to keep replaying your mother's words in your head, or give any credence to what she said to you. She's gone. Don't let her continue to control you."

Issie pulled away from Bella and wiped her face with the back of her hand, before quoting solemnly: "'The dead know not any thing . . . for the memory of them is forgotten. Also their love, and their hatred, and their envy, is now perished; neither have they any more a portion for ever in any thing that is done under the sun.'"

"Exactly," Bella said, tenderly pushing a strand of hair out of Issie's face. "Shakespeare?"

"No," Issie said, surprised. "It's from the Bible!"

The two girls broke into giggles, and there was still a slight tremor in Bella's voice when she said, "Well then, 'Amen' to that!"

9

Issie's excursion with Dr. Jordan to the Temple of the Muses bookshop was only the first of many such outings, and the couple went to the British Museum, the Egyptian Hall, and even made a return trip to Somerset House over the next week. Though he had given her his arm to lean upon on this second visit, Issie was a little disappointed when Dr. Jordan made no attempt to put his hand at her waist, or even hold her hand as she descended the stairs.

"Instead, he told me that he was relieved that there was no need to carry me down, as there had been the last time we had visited," Issie told Bella later. "What do you think he meant by that?"

"Why, merely that he's happy your health and strength have improved so much that it's no longer necessary for him to do so."

Issie considered this in silence and then began smiling; a dreamy, faraway expression on her face. Bella assumed she was once again reliving that epic moment when the doctor had swept her up into his arms, and left her to her imaginings.

Bella, too, was very busy with outings and social activities. Lord Brooke had invited her and Issie to the theatre, but Issie, though she'd been able to endure the crowds at the Royal Academy and other places around London, still did not feel like she could face the thousands who were likely to be present at Covent Garden Theatre. (Or perhaps it was Lord Brooke she was hesitant to face.) So Miss Adams and Sir Roger had been invited instead. Lord Brooke had also invited his nephews' grandmother, Lady de Ros. She was no blood relation of Lord Brooke's, as she was the mother of his sister's husband, but Lord Brooke had come to know her after his sister had married her son. And he explained to Bella that he thought she was quite lonely now that her son and daughter-in-law had died, especially when her grandsons were away at school, as they were now.

Bella was happy Lady de Ros was coming because it gave Lady Dutton a night free from her chaperoning duties. And it gave Bella a night free from Lady Dutton.

Lady de Ros looked to be about sixty-five or seventy and was slender and elegant with beautiful white hair, but she had an air of chilly reserve that was somewhat intimidating to Bella. She did not appear to smile very frequently, and Bella wondered if she was going to be much of an improvement over Lady Dutton. But then Bella remembered how

Lord Brooke had said she was lonely, and realized that this could account for her aloof manner. So Bella tried her best to ignore her feelings of inferiority and treat Lady de Ros in her usual warm and friendly fashion.

She was finally rewarded when, after they'd all been seated in the theatre box and were waiting for the play to begin, Lady de Ros turned to Bella with a slight smile and initiated a conversation. Though Bella was not particularly happy with the subject she'd chosen.

"Lady Isabelle, you have a cousin about your own age, do you not? A girl cousin?"

"Yes, I do," Bella said, a little surprised Lady de Ros would have heard of Lady Isabelle's lower-class cousin.

"What is her name?"

Bella looked over at Lord Brooke, who was seated on her other side, but who thankfully was in conversation with Sir Roger. "Arabella Grant, my lady."

"Tell me a little about her," Lady de Ros commanded. "Is she well? Did she come to town with you?"

"She is exceedingly well. And yes, she is here in town. I beg your pardon, but how did you hear of her? She lives a very quiet life in the country."

"I was acquainted with her grandparents."

"Oh, I see," Bella answered, though she did not see at all. She assumed Lady de Ros was referring to her father's parents, as she couldn't imagine this wealthy aristocrat had ever met her mother's parents, the apothecary and his wife. But then why had she said *her* grandparents and not *your* grandparents? If she'd been referring to the Stricklands, she would have known that they were Lady Isabelle's grandparents, as well.

"Well, is there nothing else you can tell me about her?" Lady de Ros asked, a little impatiently. "Is Miss Grant as pretty as you are?"

Bella smiled slightly, able to see the humor in the question, and nodding vigorously, said, "Oh, yes, she is *just* as pretty as I am. We greatly resemble each other."

She did not realize that Lord Brooke had finished his conversation with Sir Roger and was now listening to hers with Lady de Ros. "You will not get an unbiased opinion about her cousin from Lady Belle," he said with a smile. "The two are as close as sisters. Perhaps closer."

Lady de Ros smiled broadly for the first time that evening. "I am happy to hear that you value your cousin. Too many young ladies quarrel with their female relations, especially those who are close to them in age. I am sure your cousin, orphaned as young as she was, appreciates your support."

"I know she does, just as I appreciate hers," Bella answered, though she continued to wonder how Lady de Ros seemed to know so much about Arabella Grant.

The curtain rose before Lady de Ros could interrogate her further, and while Bella had been surprised to discover that this made no difference to many of the patrons who continued to chat in loud voices throughout the performance, this was Bella's first time seeing the comedy *She Stoops to Conquer,* and she was unwilling to follow their example.

Oliver Goldsmith's play had been popular for more than forty years now, so Bella had been embarrassed to admit that she had never seen or read it, and thus was totally surprised that the plot revolved around the daughter of the house, Kate Hardcastle, assuming a false identity, first as a maid, and then as a poor relation.

Apparently, Catherine had never seen the play, either, and was also surprised by its content. Marlow, the ostensible hero of the story, seemed little more than a cad to both young ladies, as he was terrified to court proper young ladies, but took liberties with women of a lower class. Since both Bella and Catherine *were* of a lower class, though had hidden this fact from their escorts that evening, they were both squirming in their seats at some of the dialogue.

The two young women did laugh loudly at the scenes that didn't remind them of their lowly background; particularly when the gentlemen had been tricked into thinking that Mr. Hardcastle's home was an inn and he was the innkeeper and they loudly criticized the dinner menu their host planned to serve.

However, Bella did not find Kate Hardcastle and Marlow's love story funny in the least. Kate was Marlow's equal in rank; their marriage had been arranged by their fathers. And Bella felt that if Kate was actually the poor relation she was pretending to be, no one would have been scheming to get her and Marlow together, or would rejoice when they finally did become engaged.

It caused Bella to wonder if she had been fooling herself all along where Lord Brooke was concerned. Noblemen were far more likely to offer women of her class a mistress-ship, rather than a marriage. In the play, Marlow told Kate: "The difference of our birth, fortune, and education, makes an honourable connexion impossible."

So Bella's laughter was forced and her applause half-hearted, and both she and Catherine wished there had been a different play scheduled that evening.

Lord Brooke was observing her closely throughout, and seemed to realize that she had mixed feelings about the evening's entertainment. "You don't seem to have enjoyed the play unreservedly. Did it remind you too much of your own situation?" he asked Bella in a lowered voice while the rest of the audience was applauding the actors as they took their bows.

"What do you mean?" Bella asked, turning to look at him and wondering if he had somehow guessed her secret after all.

"Did Mrs. Hardcastle remind you of your mother?"

Bella was so greatly relieved at his question it took her a moment to realize he was awaiting an answer, and then she had to think back on Mrs. Hardcastle's part in the play. It was true that hers was a strong personality, and she had tried to force her son and his cousin to marry each other against their will, even withholding her niece's jewels from her in an attempt to blackmail them into marriage. "Perhaps a little," Bella said, and was glad she had that excuse for disliking the play. But then she decided to tell him her true opinion. "However, I was also taken aback at the gentlemen's opinion of women who were not of their class."

Lord Brooke looked surprised for a moment, as if this aspect of the story had not previously occurred to him. Then, after he appeared to have mentally reviewed the play, his expression grew serious and he said: "Yes, Marlow is a bit of a scoundrel in that regard. I suppose Goldsmith had to have an excuse for setting up the misunderstanding between him and Kate, but it is common, unfortunately, to find that sort of attitude prevalent among gentlemen in society even today."

Bella did not reply, and after a short pause, he continued: "I find it despicable, myself. No man should force his attentions on any woman, whether she be a milkmaid or a marchioness."

Bella rewarded him with a glowing smile for this remark, but their conversation was interrupted when guests began entering the box during the intermission before the pantomime was to begin.

One of these guests was Mr. Peckham, who had given up his Cossack trousers and was once again wearing a pair of his extremely tight pantaloons. Bella thought at first his ruddy cheeks had been caused by the heat of the gaslit, crowded theatre, but realized after he turned eagerly to Catherine, at which point his cheeks grew even redder, that he was embarrassed, or bashful, or just plain excited, about seeing Catherine Adams again.

He gave the rest of them a quick greeting, bowing slightly to Bella and murmuring, "Lady Belle, good evening," before making the true reason he'd come to their box obvious. He bowed far more deeply to Catherine and bestowed an admiring glance on her before saying, *"Miss Adams,* good evening," in a reverential tone that was far different from the one he'd used when greeting the others.

Bella exchanged a glance with Lord Brooke, who had observed this unlikely sight as well, but then she had to quickly look away from him because the amused gleam in his eye almost caused her to laugh, and she had no desire to make Mr. Peckham turn even redder.

Catherine appeared startled and uncertain about Mr. Peckham's motives in addressing her, and returned his deep bow with a slight nod and a frown. She had apparently not caught on to the fact that he'd left Lady Belle's court to join hers, where he was at present its sole member.

"Miss Adams, would you care to walk with me during the intermission?" he asked, though he appeared a little deflated by her reception of him and asked this very tentatively and hesitantly, as if he expected a negative response.

But Catherine, looking from Mr. Peckham to Bella and back at him again, finally *did* understand that he had transferred his allegiance to her. And whereas if someone had asked her a day earlier her impression of Mr. Peckham it would have been a decidedly negative one, it is very difficult to hold a bad opinion of a person who so obviously admires you. Therefore, she bestowed a smile on him and said, "Thank you, I would be very glad to stretch my legs—" and then with a horrified glance around her, gasped and covered her mouth, before recovering her composure and saying: "That is, I would be pleased to take some air."

After they had left, Lord Brooke turned and said to Bella: "Her mother obviously didn't train her as well as yours did."

"There is nothing wrong with using that word," Bella said, her hackles rising in defense of poor Catherine.

"What word?" Sir Roger asked.

"It doesn't matter," Bella said, with a quick glance at Lord Brooke, who winked at her and mouthed the word "legs" in an exaggerated and comically rakish manner.

"Lord Brooke, don't be vulgar," said Lady de Ros, whose presence everyone had forgotten. Upon which command Lord Brooke obediently sat up a little straighter and begged her pardon. But it was obvious he hadn't been truly chastened, because after a moment he turned to Bella and said, "My extremities are in need of mobilization as well, if Lady Belle would do me the honor."

Bella, biting her lip in order to maintain a straight face, wondered if she should reward the wretched man by giving him what he had asked for. But then she decided to deny him would be denying herself as well. So she nodded in response and left the box with him, her hand on his arm and her head held high, and restrained her laughter until Lady de Ros was out of earshot.

Later, while they were walking in the elegant saloon that only those wealthy enough to have their own private box had access to, Bella felt again like she was living in a sort of dream. She still had not grown accustomed to all the glamour that surrounded her. The Covent Garden Theatre, rebuilt in 1809 after having burned down the year before, was a marvel to Bella. Right now they were two of a select group who promenaded in a high-ceilinged vestibule with life-size sculptures, sparkling chandeliers, marble columns, and velvet banquettes.

After politely greeting some of their acquaintance, Lord Brooke led Bella to one of those plush benches and invited her to take a seat in one corner.

"I thought we were on a mission to mobilize our extremities," Bella said, her lips in a prim smile.

"Ostensibly, that was our purpose, but I had another purpose in mind as well," Lord Brooke told Bella, placing his arm against the wall so that he effectively shielded her from view and his back was to the room.

"Oh, and what was that?" Bella asked, a little breathlessly, as her heart had taken to beating as rapidly as she imagined Issie's did when she had "palpitations."

"To speak to you privately, away from the crowds. You are too popular to suit me, Lady Belle," he said, his voice almost a caress, it was pitched so low.

"You are also very popular, Lord Brooke. A young lady might worry that you were merely toying with her affections if she found herself the target of your attentions. It is rumored you are reluctant to make any lasting commitment."

Lord Brooke frowned, his expression growing serious. "Is that what you fear, Bella?" he asked. "Is that why you are sometimes distant with me? Are you protecting yourself?"

"I—" Bella began, and then stopped, unsure what to say. Why was it that she always ended up having to answer *his* questions, when she was the one who needed answers from him? She longed to tell him what she truly feared, but she'd promised Issie to wait. "I suppose I am," she finally said, as it was true that she was protecting herself, even if it wasn't entirely for the reasons he supposed.

"You needn't do so," Lord Brooke said, putting a finger under her chin and gently tilting her face back up after she'd lowered her gaze, afraid he might read the whole truth in her eyes. "I would never hurt you."

"You cannot promise such a thing," Bella said. "No one can."

"I suppose you are right. But when I look at you, so lovely and guileless and true, I feel like I'd cut out my own heart before I caused yours a moment's pang."

Bella tried not to wince when he'd called her "guileless and true," though she did close her eyes for a moment.

"You're doing it now. Why do you withdraw from me whenever I try to express my feelings?"

"Is that what you are doing?" Bella said, opening her eyes wide. "Please proceed, then; there's nothing I'd rather hear."

Lord Brooke smiled at her response, but someone was approaching, calling his name, and his smile disappeared and he sighed. "This is neither the time nor the place," he said regretfully, before straightening and turning to greet his so-called friend, Lord Barnaby Chester.

Bella echoed his sigh, and Lord Barnaby, not usually the most sensitive of souls, began to think his presence wasn't entirely welcome.

10

Bella and Issie could not believe their London season was coming to an end and they had not received a declaration of love or an offer of marriage, or both, from their desired bridegrooms. Neither, it seemed, could Lady Dutton believe it.

On their way home from a musical concert a few nights after Bella's visit to the theatre, Lady Dutton said abruptly to her: "Lord Brooke hasn't spoken to you?"

"Spoken to me?" Bella asked, confused, as Lady Dutton had seen her and Lord Brooke in conversation just moments earlier.

"I had naturally assumed he would come to me or Lord Dutton first, before speaking to you, but this modern generation"—she made a tsk-ing sound—"they do not show proper respect for The Way Things Are Done." From the manner in which Lady Dutton said those last five words

Bella imagined them capitalized, like a proper noun. And she now understood Lady Dutton's meaning.

"No, Aunt Lucretia. Lord Brooke has not spoken to me."

"Hmph," Lady Dutton said. "And you're sure you have not done anything to give him a disgust of you? Talked to him of politics, or religion, or—God forbid—*science*?"

"I would never even *think* of discussing science with Lord Brooke," Bella said, and her irrepressible sense of humor saved her from becoming angry with Lady Dutton, or Lord Brooke, and made her want to giggle instead.

"Well, I see no reason for you to be *grinning* about it," Lady Dutton said, which caused Bella's grin to widen. "However, I am sure he intends to speak soon. Otherwise he would not have paid you such pointed attentions."

Bella didn't feel like grinning when she thought over that conversation later in the privacy of her bedchamber. She was extremely ambivalent about the end of her visit to London. On the one hand, she would finally be finished with this charade and could resume her own identity. On the other hand, if Lord Brooke did not express his love for her soon, she would leave London and never see him again anyway. From what he had said to her at the theatre, it did seem like he was fond of her, but he had made no move to seek her out privately since that night. What if she had no opportunity to tell him the truth of her identity before she returned to Fenborough Hall? Was it possible that, despite his words, this had been no more than a flirtation for him? In that case, what would it matter if she was called "Arabella Grant" or "Lady Belle"? Who would even care what her name was when she was immured in Oxfordshire? Not the cows or the milkmaids, that was for certain.

But a few days later, she and Issie were confronted with an even more horrible fate. Both girls had gone down to the drawing room that morning, as Lady Dutton had requested a meeting. They were experiencing some trepidation about what she could want, but assumed it concerned their plans for returning to Fenborough Hall.

However, according to what they learned from Lady Dutton, they were *not* returning to Fenborough Hall.

"Since Lord Dutton was appointed the primary trustee of your estate, and you will not have control of it until your marriage or until you turn five-and-twenty, we have decided to appoint a caretaker for the hall, and you, Isabelle, will go with us to our estate in Warwickshire. Your cousin will have to make her own arrangements," Lady Dutton said, casually picking up a bonbon and popping it in her mouth, with absolutely no concern for the devastation she'd just wrought.

There was a shocked silence before Bella finally spoke up. "I don't understand; I thought that my cousin and I would be going back home to Fenborough Hall. We'd much prefer to do so. Surely, that would be less bother and expense for you, Aunt Lucretia." Bella was speaking in her guise as Lady Isabelle, and Issie nodded vehemently in agreement with her words.

"You have no older female relative to chaperone you

there. We could hire one, I suppose, but it makes no sense to do so, nor does it make sense to keep an entire estate running for the comfort of one young woman, when you can stay with us, and the expense for your upkeep will be negligible. Also, I'm sure you'll be wed very soon, just as soon as Lord Brooke makes a formal offer, which should be any day now. He could not call on you if you were living unchaperoned at Fenborough Hall, but he can if you're living with me."

Both girls ignored the part of Lady Dutton's speech concerning Lord Brooke, as they were still stymied by her previous remark that Bella would not be accompanying them.

"But—what about Ara—?" Issie said, finding her voice and then remembering *she* was supposed to be Arabella. "What about me? What am I supposed to do?"

"That is not my concern. If you'd had any sense at all, you would have taken advantage of this precious opportunity to find yourself a husband. Surely, there was some foolish gentleman on the fringes of Lady Isabelle's court who could have been convinced to take her cousin instead. But no, you couldn't be bothered to secure your future and spent the last two months pampering yourself."

Issie shrank back into her chair at the harsh tone Lady Dutton had used, and though Bella knew the unkind words and the bleak fate were intended for *her*, not Issie, she also knew that it was Issie who was most harmed by such a speech, because it brought back painful memories of her mother's cruel tirades.

So Bella quickly drew Lady Dutton's attention back to herself. "When are we to leave for Warwickshire?"

"Friday," Lady Dutton answered.

It was now Wednesday. The two girls looked at each other in despair, before quickly taking leave of Lady Dutton and running up to Bella's room.

"What are we to do, Bella? She can't actually separate us, can she?" Issie asked, and she suddenly looked as pale and sickly as she had when they had first arrived in town.

"I think she can, at least for the next six years, until you turn five-and-twenty." Bella wished she'd not voiced such a thing when she saw Issie wince, as it did sound like an unbearably long period of time when spoken aloud.

But then Issie stood up straighter and a look of resolution appeared on her face. "I must convince Dr. Jordan to marry me," she said.

"Do you think—Will Lord Dutton even permit you to marry him?" Bella asked, as she now realized that Lady Strickland's death had not brought them the absolute freedom they'd assumed it had. "If you marry, you'll have to give your real name and reassume your true identity. Besides, Lord Dutton knows who we really are."

"I can elope, if necessary," Issie said, and Bella was impressed by the determination in her voice and expression. "Don't you see, Bella? If I marry, I can take possession of Fenborough Hall, and then you can come and live with us."

This did not sound to Bella like the fulfillment of all her hopes and dreams as it obviously did to Issie, but it did solve a number of problems. The first being where she was supposed to live.

"I think I must find somewhere to stay for a few weeks anyway," Bella said slowly, "because even if Dr. Jordan does want to marry you, it won't all come about instantaneously."

"Perhaps that would be wise," Issie said with a frown. "You do have *some* money, don't you?"

"I do," Bella said, and had to smile at her cousin's total ignorance when it came to financial matters, even though she felt like sobbing. But then Issie surprised her. She told her cousin to wait and disappeared for a few minutes. Bella sat obediently at her dressing table, staring unseeingly at her reflection as she tried to decide what she should do.

And then Issie ran back into the room, her hands full of a glittering array of jewelry. "Which do you think could be sold the easiest?" she asked Bella, after casually throwing jewels worth a small fortune onto the bed.

"Oh, Issie, you can't give me your jewelry!" Bella protested.

"Why not? You mean more to me than any of these *things*. If one of them can provide you with money to live on until we can be together again, that will make me far happier than these jewels ever did."

There were rings, brooches, and bracelets that were inlaid with emeralds, sapphires, rubies, diamonds, and pearls. Bella wished she or Issie were more knowledgeable about the amounts such items would fetch, but neither of them was, so Bella had to make an intuitive decision. She finally chose a ring with a huge sapphire surrounded by diamonds, reasoning that she could sell a few stones at a time or the entire thing, and hoped it would provide enough, combined with her own income, to last the six years until she could live with Issie again. (If, that is, Issie wasn't successful in convincing the doctor to marry her.) The ring also seemed too large and heavy for Issie's slender, elegant finger, so Bella reasoned it wasn't one she was likely to wear very often anyway.

She showed it to Issie and asked her opinion, but it was obvious Issie didn't care any more about that piece than she did any of the rest, and so Bella wrapped it in a handkerchief and put it under her mattress and Issie went to return the rest of the jewels to their case.

She came back again, still seething. "I will never live with Aunt Lucretia," she said, and Bella became concerned that Issie's anger might cause her to do something unwise.

"Issie, don't make any rash decisions; you may have to live with her for at least a short time."

"Never. It would be like living with my mother again. I will *not* be in a carriage headed for Warwickshire on Friday. I don't care what I have to do," Issie said, and Bella reflected that she'd never seen her timid little cousin look so ferocious. But since Bella was just as angry with Lady Dutton, she wasted no further time trying to placate Issie and instead set her mind to worrying about her own future.

That night marked one of Bella's last appearances as Lady Belle, and she was resolved to look her best. She also decided to dress more simply than the current mode. She had started her masquerade by wearing ornate court dress, complete with feathers and lappets and hooped skirts, and wanted to end the season in the opposite manner. She supposed it was somewhat metaphorical, as she was slowly stripping away her false identity and revealing more of her true self, but she wasn't thinking that deeply about it, and was instead merely following her inclination.

She wore a gown of blue-gray satin with a ruched V-neck bodice from which the skirt extended down to the ankles with no adornment, other than one very modest band of trim at the hem.

Around her neck she wore the only jewelry that was truly hers; three strands of seed pearls with a large, jeweled clasp that was made of paste. Her uncle had given it to her on her twelfth birthday and told her it had been her mother's and that she had worn it on her wedding day.

Bella ran into Lord Dutton in the hall before leaving, and after they exchanged greetings, his attention was caught by her necklace. He seemed surprised to see it, and it was the first time she had seen him drop his habitual air of noble hauteur.

"That's a pretty bauble. Where did you get it?" he asked.

Bella reflected that it was good he knew her real identity, as she was able to say honestly, "It was my mother's."

"Really?" he said, looking even more surprised, though why he would be, Bella could not fathom, unless it was because he didn't think an apothecary's daughter could afford even the simplest of jewelry.

"Yes, really," she said, standing up straighter.

He continued to look at her in a very odd manner, as if he was seeing her for the first time. And then he bowed, asked her to excuse him, and left.

Shortly afterward, the coach was ready and she and Lady Dutton left the house for their final evening out.

At the same time Bella was attending her last ball of the London season, Issie was listening to a lecture with Dr. Jordan at the Surrey Institution. It was the third in a series on the English poets given by William Hazlitt, and his subjects that evening, Shakespeare and Milton, were long dead, so could not complain about anything critical he might say of them.

Issie was too nervous to truly enjoy herself, though the subject was of genuine interest to her and the speaker was a talented one. However, the rotunda where the meeting was held was extremely crowded, and the bench she sat on was not designed to hold the number of people it currently did. While she did not mind at all that she was pushed against Dr. Jordan's side, it made her extremely uncomfortable to sit so near another strange gentleman. The doctor eventually realized why Issie was burrowing into his side and put his arm around her, using it as a buffer between her and her neighbor. This relieved some of Issie's discomfort, but the delight she took from being held in his arms reminded her of the other reason for her nervousness: she had to find some way to convince the doctor to propose marriage to her before the evening was over.

Obviously, this could not be accomplished in the middle of a lecture, though she thought that the fact he had placed an arm around her was a good start. However, she was so overwhelmed by Dr. Jordan's proximity she was paying even less attention to the speech, so that when the rowdy audience broke out in boos and hisses or applause and laughter, it startled her so much that she jumped in response. The doctor responded by stroking her arm in a soothing manner. This did nothing to calm her nerves, but did cause her to focus far more on the pleasurable tingle his caresses were causing than on the clamor of the crowd. And as the hour progressed, her concentration was centered so much on the touch of his hand that she might have been marooned with him on a deserted island for all the awareness she had of the people who surrounded them. She had unknowingly started holding her breath whenever his hand stilled, in anticipation of when his fingers might resume lightly brushing her arm again and in wonder over how those featherlight strokes could cause such a tumult inside of her.

After the lecture had ended, Dr. Jordan turned to look at Issie, and though he smiled at her, he appeared slightly self-conscious. "Did you enjoy that?" he asked, withdrawing his arm from around her, which caused Issie to shiver.

"Very much," she said, though she didn't think either of them were speaking of the lecture. They were staring silently into each other's eyes, and it wasn't until someone began to complain that the doctor was blocking the row that he and Issie began making their way out of the building.

Issie was clinging to the arm he'd given her to lean upon, but people were bumping and jostling her, so that he again put his arm around her, and she gratefully nestled into his side, placing her own arm around his waist.

When they were finally outside on the street and a little removed from the others, he tightened his arm around her before gently withdrawing it.

"I must find a hackney to take you home," he said softly. And Issie nodded in comprehension, though she felt what he was really doing was apologizing for having to leave her side.

After he had found a coach and they were both seated inside, there was an awkward silence, as if the doctor had repented of his earlier boldness and it embarrassed him. Issie could not clearly see his face; it was dark inside the carriage and he was seated on the bench across from her. She had no idea what to say or do to regain their previous intimacy, and was very aware that every turn of the coach's wheels was hastening their eventual parting unless she did something.

"I leave London on Friday," she finally blurted out.

"So soon?" he asked, and she was heartened by the obvious disappointment in his voice. She told herself she hadn't the time to be shy, and moving as cautiously as she could in the bouncing carriage, she transferred to his bench. However, she stumbled a bit when the carriage hit a rut in the road, and she would have fallen had he not caught her.

His hands were on her shoulders and she was almost sitting in his lap, and the silence seemed to hum from the tension between them. Finally, Issie said: "Dr. Jordan? Would you kiss me?"

Without a single word he instantly complied, kissing her with such passion and intensity, it was as if he had been waiting all evening for just such an invitation. Issie wondered if perhaps she had a weak heart after all, as it was pounding so fiercely she thought she might be about to expire in his arms. But then she reflected everyone had to die sometime, and she couldn't think of a better way to go. And she began kissing him back just as passionately, proving to be as quick a learner at this activity as she was in all her other studies.

He finally paused and drew back, gasping for breath, as was Issie. "Miss Grant, I beg your pardon. You are probably not strong enough for such a vigorous embrace."

But when he called her by her cousin's name, it caused Issie to suddenly remember the confession she must make. After a necessary pause spent recovering her breath, she said, "Dr. Jordan, I must tell you: my name is not Arabella Grant."

"What?" Dr. Jordan said, and though Issie could not see him, she imagined he must be extremely confused. First she threw herself into his arms, then boldly asked him to kiss her, and finally informed him she was not the lady he thought she was.

"Arabella Grant is my cousin's name, and she is using mine for the season. As you know, I was not well enough for my come-out when we first arrived in London, and that was the sole reason my aunt invited us to town. Bella and I decided it would be better for all involved if she assumed my identity and took on those exhausting social activities in my place. The substitution was merely to last the duration of our visit to London. Though, honestly, I would not care if it were to last the rest of our lives."

"I am not sure I understand. Your cousin . . . She is Lady Isabelle, is she not?"

"That is the name she has been using, but it is actually *I* that am Lady Isabelle." As soon as she'd said this, Issie worried her grammar was incorrect, and then decided it didn't matter.

"Good God, I have been kissing Lady Isabelle Grant? The daughter of a marquis? The toast of London society?"

He sounded completely appalled and Issie was surprised by his reaction. "No, of course not. You haven't been paying attention: it is my *cousin* who is the toast of London."

"Because she is an heiress to a large fortune and a palatial estate! But *you* are actually those things," Dr. Jordan said, and though he was still in darkness and she couldn't make out the expression on his face, Issie could tell from his tone of voice that he was upset for some unknown reason. Perhaps because he felt himself beneath her now that he knew her true position and assumed there was no possibility she would consider his suit. She was delighted to be able to tell him how she really felt.

"Well, yes, I thought it might be immodest of me to admit it right away, but if you were to marry me, I am not the poor orphan you believed me to be—"

"If I were to marry *you*? Marry *Lady Isabelle Grant*?" he said, as if that were the most repellant notion he had ever heard. "Ha! I'd rather die!"

Issie, who was still sitting very near to Dr. Jordan on the bench, drew back as if she'd been slapped.

"I am sorry, Miss—Lady Isabelle, that was not very polite. It's not *you* that I object to. Or at least, not when I thought you to be Miss Grant. But, you see, I have nothing but contempt for the aristocracy."

Issie did not find this explanation at all comforting, and just wanted the ride to be over so she could attain the privacy of her room and sob into her pillow. All she knew was that not only had she failed in her attempt to find an escape from her dire situation, she had also been ignominiously and resoundingly rejected. She really did not care to hear the reasons why. From the first moment she'd heard that tone of contempt she was so familiar with, she'd wanted nothing more than to escape the situation. But the doctor went into a long lecture about how families such as hers had made their wealth through profits from the slave trade or, even if they did not own plantations in the West Indies, there was a glut of child labor in England itself that they benefited from. And then there was the Inclosure Act, which Dr. Jordan said was a complete travesty of justice and had made the landowners rich at the expense of the common Englishman. While Issie had no doubt that the aristocracy was responsible for much of the corrupt and terrible crimes he was speaking of, and she held a similarly negative view of the so-called noble class, she highly doubted that her family was specifically to blame for every ill. She knew for a fact that they had not participated in the slave trade, as her father had been a staunch abolitionist. But she had no desire to defend herself. Her head was spinning, and she couldn't understand how those beautiful lips had gone so quickly from lovingly caressing hers, to issuing this fierce diatribe.

Finally, they reached Lady Dutton's townhouse and the doctor sputtered to a stop. "I beg your pardon, Lady Isabelle. I seem to have mounted my particular hobbyhorse and gone on a bit of a tirade."

Issie did not reply; she was fumbling with the carriage door and trying to exit the coach as quickly as possible.

"Here, let me help you," he said, and he opened the carriage door and jumped down before holding out his hand to help her descend. She gingerly took his fingers, wishing she needn't touch him at all, and dropped his hand as soon as she reached the ground. Then she ran for the townhouse, with him following behind, mumbling apologies and farewells that she ignored. Once she had reached the house and the door had been opened for her, she turned and closed it in his face without having said a single word since he'd stated he'd rather die than marry her.

11

Most of the *haut ton* were making plans to leave town in the next few weeks to spend the summer at their country estates, so the last ball of Bella's London season was a popular one. Catherine hadn't been invited, nor had Mr. Peckham, as they didn't fly quite so high and invitations were hard to come by. Bella was sorry not to see her friends one last time, but resolved to at least send a letter with a private goodbye to Catherine before she left London.

She knew Lord Brooke was to be at the ball, however, as he had already reserved two dances with her.

The night seemed to be passing by far too quickly to Bella, and it had a frenetic quality about it; the lights were too bright, the music too loud, the rooms too hot, Bella's laughter more nervous than genuine.

During their waltz together, Lord Brooke seemed to notice her uncertain mood, and he whisked Bella out a set of

French doors and into the gardens before she could think of refusing. Though of course she wouldn't have, even if given the choice. This was the opportunity she'd hoped for, to speak privately with Lord Brooke, and she should have been happy that it was finally happening. Instead, she was now in a state bordering on fatalistic. What did anything matter, after all? She had been a fool to think that she could escape the destiny that had been set out for her since her birth. Lady Strickland had told her so, and she would have been better off had she believed her. Instead, she had flown too close to the sun and, like Icarus, was about to lose her wings and suffer a humiliating fall.

Lord Brooke said nothing as he led her into the darker part of the gardens, eventually stopping at a stone bench. She smiled a little when she saw him wipe it off with his handkerchief before inviting her to sit. Dirtying her skirts was the least of her concerns, though she felt the ice around her heart melt a little at his chivalrous gesture.

"Now, tell me, why do you look as if you've lost your best friend? Is your cousin in good health?" he asked.

"Yes, she's well enough. I suppose I'm saddened by the fact that we leave in two days, and—I will never see you again," she said, answering him honestly. Because, of all the terrible things that were about to happen, including her separation from Issie and her need to find a place to live, the thought of never seeing Lord Brooke again ranked as the worst.

"In two days? I had no idea your departure was so soon. Forgive me, at first I alarmed you by moving too fast, and now I've gone too slow. I'm a fool," he said with a rueful smile, but Bella did not smile in return. She barely comprehended what he was saying and merely stared up at him, the moonlight reflecting off the unshed tears in her luminous blue eyes.

"Oh, Bella, of course you will see me again. I will never leave you; I never could," Lord Brooke said, and dropping down to the bench beside her, he took her in his arms.

Bella began to wonder if she were dreaming; the evening had already had a feeling of unreality about it, and this, above all else, seemed like it had to be a fantasy of her own devising. At first, he merely held her tightly, her breast pressed so closely against his that she could feel the beat of his heart and the hard plane of his chest just as she had the first time they'd met when she'd unintentionally thrown herself into his arms. She had wanted nothing more than to be back in his embrace ever since their first, eventful meeting, and now it felt as if she had come home after a very long journey. But then he pulled back and kissed her; on her cheek, her forehead, even the side of her neck, as if he was taunting her by not meeting her lips with his own. But she knew that he was always kind to her, never cruel, and that those teasing kisses were his way of asking permission, so that when he finally did touch his lips to hers she was more than willing, nay, eager, to receive them.

This kiss was far more satisfying than their first, as that one had been interrupted before they'd barely begun, and this one went on and on. Bella would not have cared if he kissed her till morning; she never wanted him to stop, but he finally drew gently away from her.

"Bella, I apologize. I should have waited till after everything was official, I suppose, but we've been promised to each other for so long, I think I can be forgiven for stealing a kiss or two," he said, with the boyish grin she usually found so appealing. But she was so shocked by what he'd just said that she had no desire to smile in return, and when he dipped his head to resume kissing her, she drew away from him.

"What did you just say?" she asked.

"That I should not have kissed you until our engagement was official? Don't worry; it was said in jest. But I promise to put a notice in the papers this week, if it relieves your mind," he said, dropping a kiss on a sensitive spot below her ear. "I'll even get a special license and we can marry immediately," he whispered into the ear he'd just kissed, and Bella, who was trembling and lightheaded from the effect of his touch and his voice and his nearness, forced herself to try to think. She put a shaking hand to his chest and held him away from her.

"Wait," she said. "You said we are promised to each other, and have been for a long time."

"Yes, more than five years now. Surely, I've waited long enough, and can be rewarded with a kiss after all this time."

Bella, still in shock, said: "You, Lord Brooke, and Lady Isabelle Grant, are contracted to marry."

"I'm not sure *contracted* is the correct word; I don't think there was ever such a formality as a contract made; but you had to know that it had been planned for us. I was sure when you made that visit to Bluffton Castle that your mother told you. She had to have told you. I cannot understand why you seem so surprised."

Bella thought back over what she knew of Issie's life since that visit. "Then why have you never made any effort to see me, even once, in the years since that meeting?"

"What was the point? I knew you would be making your come-out when you were eighteen, and we could not be married before then. I was told you had insisted upon having a London season before we married. Everything was delayed, of course, when your mother died, and I admit I felt like I'd been granted a bit of a reprieve. I wasn't fully convinced, in my callow youth, of the wisdom of an arranged marriage. To tell you the truth, I was dead set against the idea. My poor sister had been forced into one, and her marriage had been very unhappy. So I had ranted and raved that I would never submit to such a thing, and completely overlooked the benefits of such an arrangement."

"And what benefits are those?" Bella asked.

"Why, the usual things; we had a very similar upbringing and we have much in common, more than I could even list. You're the daughter of a peer and have been trained since childhood to become the wife of one. I must admit such arguments meant next to nothing to me when I was an immature young man determined not to submit to my parents' wishes, but I can see some wisdom in them now."

When Bella continued to frown at him, he seemed to realize this line of reasoning wasn't very complimentary and changed course. "And when I met you again; well, you can have no doubt that I've been assiduously and willingly courting you since the day we ran into each other at St. James's. And I've been cursing myself for having wasted all that time, after all."

He smiled lovingly at Bella, but all Bella could think was that his smile was meant for Issie, not for her; that all of it—his attentions, his compliments, his kindnesses—was intended for Issie all along, even those passionate kisses he had just given her and she'd returned so ardently. She had never been entitled to any of it; it was all as false as the identity she bore.

His smile faded the longer she stared at him in silence, and then she stood up and ran from the garden and from him. Her only small comfort was that when he called after her, it was *her* name he was calling, not Issie's.

"Bella, wait," he said.

But there was only one person Bella wished to talk to at that moment.

Issie's evening had ended much earlier than Bella's, so she'd had hours to cry into her pillow before Bella returned. And even though Issie felt as if her heart were breaking and that she would never be able to do anything so prosaic as sleep, she had just fallen into a light doze when Bella threw open the door and swept into the chamber.

"Is it true, Issie? Was a marriage arranged between you and Lord Brooke by your parents?" Bella demanded, and Issie wondered why all the consequences of her lies and omissions had come home to roost on this one particular night.

"Is it true?" Bella asked again, after Issie had sat up in bed and merely blinked in response. "You and Lord Brooke were promised to each other?"

"Yes, it's true," Issie said, and her broken heart cracked a little further when she saw the disappointment on her cousin's face.

"I don't understand. If you were already spoken for, why did you want Dr. Jordan to court you?"

"Because I foolishly thought I could escape my destiny," Issie said expressionlessly, as she had cried so much and for so long that she had now reached a state of numb acceptance and resignation. "But I should have known it was impossible."

"And you didn't think you should inform me of this little detail when I was pretending to be you?" Bella was trying her best to keep her temper under control, but she couldn't restrain herself completely, and some of her anger made itself evident in her tone of voice, and Issie winced a little at the sound of it, muted though it was.

"You don't understand. It was the most humiliating experience of my life. I wanted to forget it ever happened." Issie expelled a deep sigh before continuing. "You remember when my mother and I went to Bluffton Castle when I had just turned fourteen," she said, and Bella nodded. "I know that I'm not beautiful like you"—Bella made an instinctive protest that Issie ignored—"but I never thought myself ugly. That is, until I met Lord Brooke.

"My mother had spent the morning telling me the extent of my imperfections; that I was too much of a bluestocking, that I was an embarrassment to her, and that I didn't deserve the match she'd managed to arrange for me in spite of my many faults. So I was already feeling very awkward and ugly and belittled. But shortly after we arrived, Lord Brooke came into the room and he was . . . beautiful, the handsomest man I'd ever seen. Of course, I hadn't seen many men at all, at that point, but to give him his due, even now that I've met a number of them, I still can't deny he's a very attractive one. But then . . . I saw his expression when he caught sight of me."

Issie paused and took a shuddering breath. "I can't even put it into words, but it was as if his worst fears had been realized. That he did not find me attractive in the least, but"—Issie's voice lowered until it was almost inaudible, and she whispered the next word, as if it was too embarrassing to say aloud—"repulsive.

"I know you say he was kind to you, and I realize he didn't mean to be cruel; he probably didn't even know what his expression revealed. But it *hurt*, Bella. It injured me greatly. It made me feel that I was so unattractive no man would ever marry me by choice, and if I were ever to marry, it would only be because my mother brought it about."

"I am so sorry, Issie," Bella murmured, much of her anger having dissipated as she listened to her cousin's explanation.

"I realize he was young, as you mentioned before, and I think he's learned some compassion since; I do believe he would more carefully control his expression if we met for the first time now. And he was probably not aware how obviously his face gave his feelings away. But that was another reason I avoided participating in the London season; I knew that even though my mother was dead, Lady Dutton would make sure Lord Brooke and I fulfilled our parents' wishes, and I couldn't bear to be rejected by him a second time."

"But Lord Brooke said you *requested* a London season."

"I did, but not because I wanted one. It was a delaying tactic. I knew if I did not come up with an excuse, and one my mother would accept, I'd be dragged to the altar as soon as I turned eighteen, if not sooner. I figured that if I asked for a season it would at least delay the inevitable another year. But you, of all people, must realize I never *really* wanted one! I just wanted to avoid marriage to a man who very clearly did not want to marry me.

"That's also why I found Dr. Jordan so appealing. I thought that perhaps, since he was not titled or wealthy, he might feel my status and fortune would make up for my other defects. Little did I realize that he would feel the exact opposite," Issie said, with a wry smile. Bella, who had no knowledge of what Issie had gone through that evening, ended up kicking off her satin slippers and climbing into bed beside her as she told Bella of her terrible night, crying again as she did so, even though she had been so sure she had no tears left. Bella comforted her and murmured to her and proved once again to be her only refuge, as she had been their entire life.

"And so I suppose I will marry Lord Brooke after all," Issie said, after she had pulled herself together and finally stopped crying. "I told you, Bella, I will do anything to avoid going to live with Aunt Lucretia. And then, if I marry Lord Brooke, I will have a home of my own and you can live with us and my aunt can't separate us. Besides, I'm prettier now than I was at fourteen, and he's much kinder than I remembered. I studied his expression when we met at the park and he did not look repulsed by me at all."

Issie yawned, and her heavy lids closed, so that she didn't see the stricken look on her cousin's face. "Dr. Jordan may have broken my heart, but I think he is probably correct that a person should not marry outside of their social class. We would have most likely been miserable," she said, with a last little gasping sob. "I would have never suspected that he's as prideful as my mother was, but in the opposite way." And then she yawned again and went to sleep.

And Bella went to her own chamber; not to sleep, but to plan what she was to do with the rest of her life.

12

It was past three in the morning when Issie had finally gone to sleep, and she was still sleeping soundly when Bella looked in on her at nine.

Bella watched her cousin for a moment while she slept, trying to imprint an image on her mind to recall later. Issie hardly looked any older than she had when Bella had first arrived at Fenborough Hall, with traces of tears on her puffy cheeks and her eyelashes matted from weeping. So innocent, so fragile, and so easily wounded. Poor little Issie.

Bella said a short prayer for Issie's happiness, wiping away the inevitable tears that she couldn't prevent from falling at the thought of their separation. She loved Issie so very much, despite the pain she was causing Bella by marrying the man she herself loved, and Bella would carry that secret to the grave before she wrecked Issie's chance of happiness with him. But neither could she live with Issie and Lord Brooke after their marriage.

She left the house a little before ten, carrying a small valise. One of the footmen found her a hackney, and she took it to the Bell and Crown coaching inn where she paid for a room for the night. She then went to Rundell, Bridge and Rundell and sold two of the diamonds in the ring that Issie had given her. After returning to the inn, she wrote a letter to Issie and gave it to a servant to deliver, and then had a dinner tray sent to her room. However, she found she was so dejected that she could barely eat and realized she would have done better to save her money. She had no doubt that she would eventually need it.

Two gentlemen arrived on the Duttons' doorstep shortly after Bella had left, both requesting an audience with Lady Isabelle. They were invited inside by the butler, where they looked each other over surreptitiously and nodded unsmilingly in acknowledgment of the other's presence.

Nancy, who happened to be crossing through the hall shortly after they had been admitted, saw Dr. Jordan standing there, assumed he had an established appointment with the young lady, and told the butler that she would escort him above stairs. She had not heard him ask for "Lady Isabelle," nor would she care if she had. She took him to the door of the sickly young lady he had visited in the past, whose real name only the good Lord knew.

Lord Brooke watched jealously as the doctor followed

the maidservant up the stairs, and wished it had been that easy for *him* to gain an audience with Bella. He was also dismayed to find Bella's description of the man was all too accurate. He *was* surprisingly handsome. And he had an air of intelligence and competence that heightened his good looks.

Lord Brooke waited impatiently while his card was taken to Lady Dutton, wondering if the doctor was a serious rival for Bella's affections after all. It was odd he was there to visit "Lady Isabelle," not her cousin. He hoped Bella was not ill. Or perhaps Dr. Jordan was visiting Miss Grant and had asked for Bella because she was chaperoning them? That would make sense, though he could just be fooling himself.

The butler returned after what seemed an interminable amount of time to tell Lord Brooke that the ladies were not yet receiving and that he should return in two hours.

"The doctor is still with Lady Isabelle?" Lord Brooke asked, though he knew that he was and that it was none of his business. Still, the man had been up there a good ten minutes with no chaperone that Lord Brooke knew of, unless Bella's cousin was with her. The flighty maid had come back down the stairs soon after she'd taken the doctor up, and Lady Dutton was probably still abed.

"I am not at liberty to say" was the butler's reply, and Lord Brooke left, frustrated he'd been unable to see Bella, and wondering how he was going to survive the next two hours.

He had stayed up most of the night, cursing his stupidity,

and wishing he could relive those moments with Bella in the garden so that he could do things differently. He'd been so overcome by the strength of his feelings for her; so bemused by the touch, and scent, and beauty of Bella, that he had hardly been aware of what he was saying. He thought she had merely been concerned with the propriety of the situation, and so sought to reassure her that he meant to marry her. It wasn't until later that he realized he'd never told her that he was only complying with their mothers' scheme because he had fallen in love with her. He had never even told her that he *did* love her! Nor had he actually proposed, but had just taken it for granted that she was amenable to an arranged marriage that he had not even wanted himself before he had come to know and love her. He didn't think he could have handled the situation any worse if he had been trying to do so.

Nor had he discovered what her feelings were for him. He felt that she reciprocated his feelings, though he was uncertain to what degree. Certainly, it had appeared as if she loved him when she was sweetly and ardently returning his kisses—though that was not something he could think about for any length of time without going weak in the knees. However, these last few months his interactions with her had felt somewhat like a choreographed dance, where every time he would step forward she would immediately take a step back.

That was also why he had waited so long to speak to her about marriage. Not only had he felt there was no need to hurry, as they had been unofficially engaged for years, but he had also not wanted her to feel like he was putting her under too much pressure, as her mother had. He had wanted them to have a real courtship, something which most participants in an arranged marriage were deprived of.

But it was odd that Bella had seemed as if she was unaware of the plans their mothers had made for them. Had she assumed that the arrangement had ended with the death of her mother? Should he have plainly spoken of it when she first arrived in town? But at that point he was unsure if he was willing to submit to the arrangement himself. And he had made oblique references to it on their first drive and at the Royal Academy, and both times she had not seemed interested in pursuing the topic.

His thoughts chased themselves around and around in his head until he thought he would go mad, while the clock seemed to stubbornly refuse to advance those one hundred twenty minutes—seven thousand two hundred seconds—until he could see her again.

Nancy had knocked on Issie's door, announced that the doctor was there to see her, let him in, and immediately left, shutting the door behind him.

Issie, who had been soundly sleeping before Nancy's knock, was horrified Dr. Jordan had found her in such a disheveled state. She couldn't believe he was there, and closed her eyes at the sight of his handsome face.

But her bedraggled, tear-ridden, haggard countenance affected the doctor far more than the sight of her with her hair elaborately arranged and her cheeks and lips rouged ever could. The affection and attraction and admiration that had been germinating in his heart suddenly burst into the full flower of love. He deeply regretted his words of the previous evening and had gone there with the intention of offering a heartfelt apology, and had been surprised to be ushered into her bedchamber. (He wasn't sure that she would agree to see him at all.) But upon seeing how heart-broken and distraught she looked, he rushed to her bedside to pull her into his arms and press kisses on her rumpled hair, with absolutely no concern for the gross impropriety of what he was doing.

"Please, *please* forgive me, my dearest," he said, as he still had no idea what he was supposed to call her. But if Issie had any objection to this form of address she did not mention it. Indeed, it was a good thing she was only half-awake and not fully coherent, as she would not have forgiven Dr. Jordan so easily had she had time to remember how deeply his words had hurt her the evening before. But in her dazed state she submitted docilely to his caresses and endearments, and after a moment began to cooperate a little *too* enthusiastically, considering the fact that the two of them were in a bed together and were not yet married or even engaged.

Thankfully, the doctor came to his senses and pulled away. "My dear—" he said, and then, as if realizing he would need to use her name at some point, asked, "May I call you Isabelle?"

"Please, call me Issie," she replied, leaning in for another kiss. Dr. Jordan could not bear to disappoint her, or himself, and there were another few kisses given and received before he pulled away again, this time to get up and walk a discreet distance away from the bed.

"Issie, you may call me James," he said, pushing his hair out of his eyes and making other adjustments to his appearance in an effort to appear more composed and less shaken than he actually was.

"James," Issie said.

James was so charmed by the sight and sound of his name on her lips that he was overcome by the desire to kiss her again. However, firmly resisting the temptation, he said, "Issie, I was very wrong last night to speak to you the way that I did. Please say you will forgive me."

This statement caused Issie to become fully alert, and some of her anger was rekindled at this reminder. "You were very unkind to me," she said.

"I will never be so again," he promised. "I had not realized until I considered it later that my prejudice *against* the aristocracy was as deep as their prejudice against the lower classes. It is a grave fault, and I will work diligently to overcome it. I admired you greatly when I thought you were Miss Grant; indeed, you are the most intelligent and interesting and enchanting woman I have ever met, and you were Lady Isabelle that entire time. So obviously your title is irrelevant."

Issie nodded her head in acceptance of his apology in a

very dignified gesture that, though she did not know it, made her appear every inch the grande dame. James, observing her with a wry smile, gave a mental shrug. He loved this woman, in spite of her aristocratic blood, and, if he were honest with himself, found her little refined mannerisms quite adorable.

"Issie, I know I'm considered far beneath you and from the world's viewpoint couldn't, and probably shouldn't, aspire to your hand, but"—and at this point he kneeled on the floor beside her bed—"will you marry me? I promise to love you most tenderly for the rest of our lives together."

Issie, her eyes bright with unshed tears, gestured for him to get up. "Please, do not kneel to me, James. It will only further your negative opinion of the upper classes," she said, with a smile that glowed as brightly as her eyes did.

James smiled back, but got to his feet a little uncertainly. After all, she still hadn't said yes.

"Tell me before I answer you: Do you think I'm pretty?" she asked shyly.

"No," he said promptly. "I think you are the most beautiful and desirable woman I've ever met. Particularly after you began eating beefsteak," he added, as she was looking a tad pale that morning and he thought a reminder might be in order.

"I would be honored to marry you, James," she said, after she had swallowed the lump in her throat. The doctor expelled a quite audible sigh of relief. "Really," Issie continued, "you should be glad you're marrying a wealthy aristocrat, since we can work together to ensure my fortune is used for the benefit of the poor. Because, though I did not appreciate the *manner* in which you said what you did, I strongly agree with the principles that caused you to say it. I find your desire to fight injustice and corruption very *noble*," she said with a teasing smile.

She held out her arms to him, but he did not return to her side, even though her little speech had made him want to kiss her till they were both breathless. "Issie, I promise to explain to you the reason why after we are married, but at this present moment I do not think it wise if we continue to embrace while you're wearing a flimsy nightdress and lying in bed."

"Yes, I remember that you were quite disappointed to find me waiting for you in bed the last time you visited me in my room," Issie said.

"Believe me, I will feel much differently after we are married," the doctor said with a grin.

Since it was now Thursday and the next day Issie was supposed to leave London with her aunt, she felt there was no time to waste and told James they should elope that very afternoon.

He was inclined to argue with her at first, as he felt they should at least try to get her relatives' permission before taking such a step. But when she explained that her aunt would insist that she marry Lord Brooke, who he realized was the very handsome, expensively dressed gentleman he'd seen waiting for "Lady Isabelle" in the hall, he quickly came around to her way of thinking and went to see about hiring a post chaise for the trip to Gretna Green.

Issie went to Bella's room to tell her what was happening and was disappointed that she did not appear to be in the house, but neither was she concerned by her absence. Bella frequently went to ride or walk in Hyde Park, or she might have gone to make her goodbyes to Catherine Adams. Issie hoped Bella would return before she left for Gretna Green, but jotted off a quick note just in case she did not. She also packed a trunk and retrieved her jewel case, though when she checked she was relieved to find she had quite a bit of cash on hand. And though she did not know how much it cost to fund a trip to Gretna Green, she felt that a hundred pounds was probably sufficient.

She called a footman to take her trunk downstairs, explaining to him that Dr. Jordan would be arriving with a chaise and he should give the trunk to him.

After another hour went by and Issie realized that Bella wouldn't be back in time for her to say goodbye, she left the note she'd written on Bella's bed and made her way down the stairs and to the back of the house just as the chaise Dr. Jordan had hired pulled up.

Lord Brooke arrived just moments before the doctor did, giving his card to the butler, who promptly ushered him into the drawing room.

There he was forced to wait at least ten minutes before Lady Dutton finally made an entrance. During this time, though he did not know it, Issie's trunk was secured to the post chaise and she and the doctor drove off on their journey to Gretna Green and the beginning of their life together.

"It's about time you called," Lady Dutton greeted Lord Brooke. "I imagine you're here to discuss the wedding arrangements. You certainly left it to the very last minute. Everyone who is anyone is leaving town."

"Good afternoon," Lord Brooke said, ignoring Lady Dutton's words. "I am actually here to speak to Lady Isabelle. In private," he added.

"You mean you still haven't spoken to her?" Lady Dutton asked in exasperation.

"I have spoken to her. I just neglected to get her acceptance."

"You don't need it. It's been understood these past five years. I honestly don't understand why you two aren't married already. It should have been done while my niece was alive to witness it. Still, Elizabeth did promise the girl a season, and I did my best to fulfill that promise," Lady Dutton said, before poking her head out the door to tell the butler to ask Lady Isabelle to come down.

"She is not in the house, milady," the butler replied.

"Are you sure? It's not that sickly cousin of hers that has left? She was to be gone by tomorrow."

"Both the young ladies are gone. They left earlier today, one with a valise and one with a trunk," the butler said.

Lord Brooke made an exclamation of shock but Lady Dutton waved him to silence. "He's merely confused the two girls. Happens to me all the time. Miss Grant was moving on to another situation."

"What situation; where?" Lord Brooke asked.

"How should I know? That's no concern of mine. She could not continue to batten on Lady Isabelle for the rest of her life," Lady Dutton said, oblivious to the look of shocked disgust Lord Brooke directed at her, and turned to address the butler again. "Wilson, was it Miss Grant who left?"

"It is as I told you, milady. One young lady left this morning, and the other ten or fifteen minutes ago; but both are gone."

"And they both took baggage with them?" Lord Brooke asked the butler.

"Yes, milord."

"I do not understand," Lady Dutton said, frowning. "Lady Isabelle knew we were going to Warwickshire tomorrow. I informed her of it myself just yesterday."

"Is that when you also informed Miss Grant she couldn't continue to 'batten on Lady Isabelle' and should find a different situation?" Lord Brooke asked contemptuously. "It's obvious that they chose to leave rather than be separated." Lord Brooke turned back to the butler. "Could you check their rooms? Perhaps one of them left a message."

He furiously paced the drawing room while he waited, trying to think of a plan of action should there be no note found, but very soon the maidservant he'd seen earlier ran in, clutching a folded piece of paper.

She was about to hand it to Lady Dutton, but Lord Brooke intercepted her, quickly opening and reading it himself.

Dr. Jordan and I are going to Gretna Green to be married. You should travel to Fenborough Hall and we will meet you there after we return. He truly loves me, and I love him, and I need not marry Lord Brooke.

Lord Brooke felt as if someone had punched him in the gut, and he did not resist when Lady Dutton pulled the letter from his grasp.

"It's hard to read; I am not sure why she writes with such a cramped hand, but does she say she went to Gretna Green with a doctor?" Lady Dutton said, squinting at the note she held.

"Yes," Lord Brooke said, though it was an effort for him to say anything at all. If he had been alone he felt as if he could have cried. The first and only other time he had done so as an adult was when his sister had died.

"You must go after them!" Lady Dutton said. "Hurry, you could still catch them!"

Lord Brooke did not respond, but turned and left the room, snatching up his gloves and hat from a table in the hallway. Lady Dutton followed him. "You're going after them?" she asked eagerly.

"No, Lady Dutton, I am not. You read her note. She was so eager to escape marriage to me that she eloped with another man. And she said she lov—" His voice wavered a little on the word, and he cleared his throat before completing the sentence: "She loves him."

"What does that matter! She is throwing herself away on a doctor when she might have married an earl!"

Lord Brook didn't trust himself to speak and walked out of the townhouse, ignoring Lady Dutton as she continued to insist he go after them.

13

Bella's letter was never delivered to Issie, and it sat on a silver plate in the Dutton townhouse for months, until Lady Dutton herself threw it into the fire the next time she returned to town.

Nor had Bella seen Issie's letter informing her of her elopement with Dr. Jordan. Therefore, as Bella made the trip to her grandfather's apothecary shop, she was tormented by thoughts of Issie's marriage to Lord Brooke, along with half-formed ideas of somehow stopping it, for the entire journey.

It might have been just as well that she was kept preoccupied by such morose thoughts, since she wore such a shuttered, unhappy expression that the few men who attempted to harass her along the way soon desisted. They found it disconcerting when Bella looked right through them as if she didn't see them, which she didn't.

Her last stop was at an inn in Banbury, and she tiredly got off the stagecoach twelve hours after she first got on it and went to ask the innkeeper about hiring a conveyance to take her to her grandfather's village.

This was only her second time traveling such a long distance, and her first time traveling completely alone, but she was no longer a society belle. She was now of a class of persons who must work for a living, and chaperones and maidservants and private carriages were things of the past.

Not that she planned to seek a position just yet. Her plan was to help her grandfather at his apothecary for a few weeks or months, while she figured out what to do.

She only hoped he was still alive.

Bella had diligently corresponded with her maternal grandmother until she had passed away three years ago, but her grandfather was not as avid a correspondent, and had only written to her once in the past three years, and that had been more than two years ago. Bella had never met either of her maternal grandparents in person, or at least not since she'd been old enough to remember it. They would never have thought of paying her a visit while she lived with Lady Strickland, who would probably not have received them if they *had* called. And Bella had never been permitted to visit them, either, though they lived no more than twelve miles from Fenborough Hall.

She was grateful that they had exchanged letters, though, because she knew exactly where to find her grandfather. At least, she hoped she did.

She was extremely relieved when the carriage turned down Rockston's high street and she saw the sign advertising her grandfather's shop. The summer days were long, so even though it was past seven in the evening and she'd been traveling since before daybreak, the sun had not yet set. So she was able to clearly read the wooden sign that hung over the shop door:

PERRY, APOTHECARY & ACCOUCHEUR
Chemist & Druggist

But after she'd paid the driver and walked into the shop, she was dismayed when a young man barely her own age came out of the back room. He looked as surprised to see her as she was to see him.

"Oh, I beg your pardon," Bella said. "I was looking for my grandfather, Randolph Perry."

"*You* are Mr. Perry's granddaughter?" the young man said, looking Bella up and down in a manner that she did not really appreciate. But his gaze seemed more astounded than admiring, and Bella realized that she was wearing one of her London walking dresses and bonnets and probably didn't at all resemble the granddaughter of a village apothecary, even though she'd selected her plainest ensemble and removed most of its fancy trimmings.

"I am. Where might I find my grandfather?" Bella asked, making her best attempt to imitate Lady Strickland's haughty manner, though she was not entirely successful. Still, the gaping boy stood up a little straighter and told her to follow him.

He led her through a cluttered workshop and storage room filled with vats and stoves and bottles, where the tinctures and ointments were obviously prepared. Bella looked around curiously, but the young man was walking quickly and she didn't have time to take much in if she wanted to keep up. They exited the building into a large herb garden at the back and followed a path to a small cottage.

The boy knocked at the door of the cottage. Someone shouted something from behind the door that Bella could not hear, but the young man opened the front door just wide enough to stick his head in and shout back:

"There's a young lady to see you, Mr. Perry. She says she's your granddaughter."

A moment later a cherubic-looking gnome of a man with a huge smile on his face swung the door open and said: "Arabella! What a marvelous surprise!"

"Grandpapa," Bella said, grasping the hand he'd held out to her and blinking back the moisture that came to her eyes at his warm welcome. He was beaming and hopping up and down in his excitement and squeezing her hand, before it occurred to him that they were still standing on his doorstep.

He then ushered her into the house, insisting that she give him her valise to carry and calling for the housekeeper. And it was actually *her*—little, insignificant Arabella Grant—that he was excited to see, not "Lady Belle." Perhaps she'd been mistaken in thinking it was with Lord Brooke that she belonged. Perhaps she'd finally come home.

Unfortunately, this feeling of belonging did not last very long. While her affection for her grandfather and his for her continued to grow, she couldn't say she developed the same fondness for her new life.

The young man she'd met when she'd arrived was her grandfather's apprentice, Jack Dixon. He was the first fly in the ointment (which was quite a serious analogy to use when one worked in an apothecary). He had promptly fallen in love with Bella and was making a complete nuisance of himself. Especially since there was very little Bella could do to avoid him, as when he wasn't sitting around the dining table with her for meals, they were working together in the apothecary, or attending church together, or he was following her into the garden when she went to weed or harvest the herbs.

The second problem was the vicar, Mr. Goddard. Bella realized most young women would not label him a problem, as he was considered quite a catch by the village maidens. This was partly because of his financial situation, which was very comfortable. He had been appointed to *two* livings: that of vicar in her grandfather's parish and also in another, ten miles away. This meant he collected two salaries, while his curate performed the lion's share of his duties at the other church. Mr. Goddard was the recipient of such bounty because he was very well connected, his father was one of the Wiltshire Goddards, and he was frequently invited to dinner at the home of his patron, a wealthy lord. He was also quite handsome, and many of the ladies in the congregation, single or not, would sigh when he counseled them from the pulpit, hearing very little of what he was actually saying. Bella wished she was similarly distracted when he spoke because, while Issie might scoff at Bella's lack of Bible knowledge, Bella quickly concluded that she knew more than Mr. Goddard did.

Because of his situation, he could look fairly high for a bride—certainly higher than the granddaughter of an apothecary—and would have probably considered Bella beneath his notice were she not so attractive, and if she did not dress so stylishly. It was obvious when he gazed down from the pulpit during Sunday sermons and compared the women looking back at him that Bella's wardrobe came from London, and that she had an air of sophistication that set her above the village girls. He'd also discovered that her father was the second son of a marquis. But though that did make the prospect of marriage with Mr. Perry's granddaughter more palatable, he also found it satisfying that the object of his attentions *was* of lower social standing than he was, as he was able to display his own nobility of character by condescending to woo someone beneath him. And he made sure Bella was aware of his magnanimity in stooping so low.

Thus Bella had a nineteen-year-old country bumpkin following her around all day at home, and a thirty-year-old patronizing sycophant calling on her nearly every morning except for the Sundays he delivered his weekly sermon, during which time he stared at her so intently that she became extremely uncomfortable.

What particularly bothered Bella was that these were the type of men she should have been viewing as potential husbands, and yet she couldn't help comparing them to Lord Brooke, to whom they obviously could not compare. Had she been so corrupted by her life in a higher sphere, that she now felt herself superior to the men of her own social class?

Bella knew, too, that it would please her grandfather if she made a match with either of the two men, since if she moved into the vicarage she would be living within walking distance of him, and if she married his apprentice he could leave the running of the apothecary to her and Jack and they could all live together until his death. And either match would also solve the problem of where Bella was supposed to live, now that she could no longer live with Issie. After all, her grandfather was past seventy and wouldn't live forever.

However, more than anything else, Grandpa Perry wanted Bella to be happy, and it did not escape his notice that she grew increasingly less so as the weeks wore on. One afternoon, nearly a month after she'd arrived, he sent Jack off on an errand and asked Bella to sit with him in the drawing room.

"Bella, child, what is bothering you?"

"What could be bothering me?" Bella asked.

"Oh, any number of things, I suppose. I was young once,

too, you know," he said with a smile. "If you're distressed by the attentions of those two young men, I can warn them off; just say the word. I haven't already done so because plenty of young ladies seem to be pining for the good vicar. And as for Jack, well, the boy's not very polished and perhaps a little young to be thinking of marriage, but time will cure many of his faults."

"I know, and I wish I *could* like one of them well enough to marry. I would be happy to have my future decided and be able to settle so near you. But I keep comparing them to another gentleman I knew—someone I did admire—and I realize I don't have even a smidgeon of the tender feelings for either of them that a woman should have for the man she chooses for her husband."

"Why did you not marry that man?"

"He was affianced to my cousin. Besides, I was not worthy of him," Bella said.

"I do not believe that," her grandfather said. "I'm sure you're worthy of any man you set your heart on."

Bella smiled at him and reached out to briefly squeeze his hand. "But you're obviously prejudiced in my favor."

"Is it because you're my granddaughter that you feel you're not worthy of him? Is he a nobleman?"

"Oh, Grandpapa, do not say such a thing; I'm very proud to be your granddaughter. But yes, he is an earl, and as such would not choose someone like me for his wife. Even Mr. Goddard has his doubts about whether I'm good enough for him," Bella said with a wry smile.

She was concerned when her grandfather didn't return

her smile, but frowned instead. She hoped she hadn't hurt him by telling him what she had. But then he sighed and began explaining what was really bothering him.

"You're so much like your mother. She was like a rare and beautiful bird that could not be caged. And I never told her the truth about herself. I regretted I had not done so, after it was too late. But who would have thought we would lose her so soon? She was only a few years older than you, you know, when she died. And your little brother died with her. I always wondered if I had been there . . . if they'd had an experienced doctor or midwife . . . Oh, well," the old man said, shaking himself out of his reverie and looking alert once again. "Princess Charlotte died in childbirth, so I suppose it can happen to any woman, princess or peasant.

"But I apologize my dear, I've strayed from the point. What I did not tell your mother is that, though my wife and I loved her like our own, she was not, in fact, the daughter of an apothecary. And though I wish I could have kept her here with me, and I wish the same for you, she was as entitled to marry the son of a marquis as any young woman making her curtsy at St. James's Palace."

"What? I don't understand . . ."

"Though I suppose they would have held the manner of her birth against her, had they known. She was born on the wrong side of the blanket, you see. However, your case is entirely different. Your parents *were* legally married, and your grandparents are both members of the peerage."

"My grandparents—" Bella said, looking at the man she'd thought to be her grandfather in shock.

He heaved another great sigh. "I was being selfish, I suppose, not telling you sooner. But your grandmother and I did feel your mother belonged to us, from the moment she was placed in our arms as a wee bawling baby. I delivered her, you see. Her mother couldn't keep her, and when she entrusted her to our care it felt like a . . . gift from heaven, especially since we couldn't have any children of our own. And you're so like her. I wanted to believe you truly were my granddaughter. To keep you beside me if I could."

Bella was so shocked she didn't know what to say. She had so many questions, but she was also disappointed that she wasn't actually related to this kindly man she'd grown to love. "Don't worry. You won't be rid of me so easily," she finally said, and was relieved when he smiled.

"I'm glad to hear it. And you're welcome to stay with me until I die. I'll leave you the cottage, too, so you'll always have a place to live, though that might be awkward if Jack does eventually take over the shop. But we'll worry about that later. For now, I do think you should meet your real grandmother."

"She's still alive?" Bella asked, surprised.

"She was a few weeks ago. She just came back to her country estate from London. And she lives only ten miles away. I could take you there, if you would like to meet her."

"Yes, I would like to meet my grandmother," Bella said. "If she's agreeable to it, that is. She may not want her secret revealed. After all, she's kept it successfully for, what? Forty years now?"

"True enough. I'll send her a letter asking if she'd like to meet you."

Little did Bella know that she had already met her.

Grandpa Perry sent a letter to Bella's grandmother that very day, asking permission to bring Bella to meet her, and after receiving an affirmative response, he hired a carriage and they were on their way a few days later.

Bella hadn't even asked her grandmother's name, as it never occurred to her that she might be acquainted with her. Though on the drive, Grandpa Perry did tell Bella other details of her grandmother's life.

"She was married at seventeen to a much older man and bore him a son before she was widowed. Then she fell in love with your grandfather, who was unfortunately already married."

Bella's eyes grew large at this statement, but she was careful not to express any judgment. However, her grandfather could obviously read her expression. "I do not approve of adultery, either, but unfortunately the nobility live by a different set of standards than the rest of us. And 'where there is marriage without love, there will be love without marriage.'"

Bella wondered briefly if Lord Brooke would be faithful to poor Issie and then quickly banished the thought. When she didn't reply, Grandpa Perry continued his story:

"Apparently, the man she loved was trapped in an

unhappy, unfruitful marriage, and he believed himself incapable of siring children. However, it turned out it was his wife who was infertile, which became obvious when your grandmother found herself expecting his child, with no husband to provide it with a name. So she retired to a cottage on the grounds of her country estate and called on an accoucheur from a short distance away to deliver her baby. And that's what brought first your mother, then you, into my life."

Bella smiled at him, relieved that her mother had found such a loving family when the outcome could have been far different. "What is my grandmother's name?" she asked idly, thinking it made little difference but that she'd learn it soon enough anyway.

"She is the Dowager Viscountess de Ros."

"Lady de Ros!" Bella said, surprised. "Why, I have met her."

"And she told you nothing of her relationship to you?"

"She did not know I was Arabella Grant at the time." Bella then explained to her grandfather the masquerade that she and her cousin had participated in during the London season, which she had not told him about before, preferring to leave it all behind her when she left London. Still, now that a month had gone by, she was able to give a condensed version of the tale composedly enough. Though she did feel a painful wrenching when she told him of her final days in London.

"I knew Issie would be happier with Lord Brooke than she would be with her aunt, who would treat her in the same harsh, critical way her mother had. I couldn't expose her to that, Grandpapa," Bella said earnestly, as if to convince herself as much as him. Because she'd had second, third, and fourth thoughts about the wisdom of leaving like she had, without telling Issie how she felt about Lord Brooke, or telling Lord Brooke her true identity. Though at the time she hadn't even known her *true* identity. She wondered what Lord Brooke would think if he discovered his nephews' grandmother was also her grandmother? But more than anything she wondered if he had still agreed to marry Issie once he'd discovered she was not the woman he thought she was. Bella couldn't help hoping, no matter what she'd said about Issie being better off married to Lord Brooke, that they would not actually make it to the altar.

"I doubt Lord Brooke would agree to marry your cousin after having courted you, my dear." Apparently, Grandpa Perry's thoughts were running along similar lines.

"I don't know. He sounded as if he'd come to believe in the wisdom of making an arranged marriage."

"After he fell in love with you."

"I am not so sure that he did," Bella said. "I hoped that he had, but he believed me to be his fiancée from the moment we first met. Maybe he was just courting me because that was what was expected of him."

"I find that hard to believe. But we will discuss this later. We have arrived."

Bella was startled to find that this was true, as the carriage had stopped at an elaborate gate, which was opened by the gatekeeper. Bella was suddenly panic-stricken, and not just because she was going to have to confess to that intimidating, distinguished noblewoman—who was her grandmother!—that she'd met her under a false name while masquerading as her cousin. She was also nervous at the thought that Lord Brooke was a frequent visitor to this place. What if he was here at this very moment? What would she say?

Fortunately—or unfortunately; Bella was so confused she wasn't sure what she wanted—when she asked the butler if Lord Brooke was in residence, she was told he was not. But Lady de Ros was at home to them and they were soon admitted to her presence.

Her home was just as intimidating as she was, and Bella was too distracted by the grandeur of the drawing room they'd just entered to immediately give her grandmother her attention. Bella had grown accustomed to more humble surroundings over the past few weeks while living with Grandpa Perry. She was looking around, wide-eyed, at the grand salon while her grandmother greeted her "grandfather."

When she finally did look their way, her grandfather gestured for her to come forward, and she obediently did so, curtsying before Lady de Ros. She couldn't ever imagine calling this regal woman Grandmama.

Lady de Ros seemed as distracted as Bella, and barely looked at Bella when she curtsied before her. She merely nodded her head in acknowledgment, her eyes downcast, and finally said, "Please be seated."

"My lady, I must start by making a confession—" Bella

said, only to stop short when the older lady winced and held out her hand.

"*You* must make a confession. That's rich—" And then she finally looked Bella in the face and stopped mid-sentence, her brow wrinkled. "Wait, have I not met you before?"

"Yes, my lady, that is what I must confess to you. We met in London, at the theatre with Lord Brooke. But you were told my name was—"

"Lady Isabelle," Lady de Ros finished. "Why did you pretend to be your cousin?"

Bella gave a brief explanation of the reason, and was surprised when the first question Lady de Ros asked was: "Does Lord Brooke know?"

"I did not tell him. I assume he knows now, as he informed me before I left London that he was affianced to Lady Isabelle."

"Well, at least I'm not the only one who has been guilty of deception, though yours pales in comparison with mine," Lady de Ros said with a twisted smile. And then her smile faded and she once again dropped her gaze from Bella's, and in a very tentative, humble manner that did not fit at all the image Bella had of her, she said: "You are willing to forgive me, then?" Bella's heart was touched, and she rushed from her seat to drop on the sofa next to her grandmother and grab her hands.

"Forgive you? For making sure my mother had a loving, secure home when you could not keep her? For giving her to a man who cherished and loved her as if she were his own and accepted me just as readily? I would rather thank you," Bella told her, and her grandmother dropped her head on Bella's chest and wept.

A week later, Bella was living with Lady de Ros, though she still wasn't calling her Grandmama, as it would have raised too many awkward questions. They eventually decided to tell people that Bella was a distant relation who had come to serve as Lady de Ros's companion, which was essentially true. However, the older lady insisted that Bella address her less formally, so the two had finally agreed on "Rossie." (Though Bella felt very awkward the first few times she used it, as it seemed so dreadfully *in*formal.)

Lady de Ros had invited Bella to live with her the very day her grandfather had brought her there, and though Bella knew it saddened her grandfather that she was leaving him, she thought he'd probably foreseen that very thing when he'd arranged for them to meet. Lady de Ros had also made it clear that he was welcome to visit "their" grandchild at any time, and he was coming to dinner that same week.

It was a huge relief to Bella to escape her two annoying suitors, and to have a place to live indefinitely. Though it seemed she wouldn't always be living at the family's main estate.

"I removed to the dower house when my son married, but after my daughter-in-law died I moved back, so that my grandsons would have someone to come home to on their holidays from school. But when my eldest grandson marries, I will again remove to the dower house. And you will be welcome to come with me. That is, if you are not married yourself by then."

Bella just murmured her thanks, as she had no desire to discuss her dismal marital prospects.

"Where are your grandsons now?" Bella asked, as it occurred to her there was still the danger of Lord Brooke paying a visit when they came home.

"They're in the Lake District. My eldest grandson fancies himself a poet," Lady de Ros said with a smile. Bella suddenly realized that Issie was no longer her only cousin, that she now had two new cousins, though they were not quite as closely related to her, as they were once-removed or something of the sort. Her family relationships through Lady de Ros were a little confusing, and she hadn't yet taken the time to figure them out.

"Is Lord Brooke with them?" Bella asked as casually as she could manage, though her heart rate had accelerated somewhat.

"I don't think so. I believe he is at his own estate, Bluffton Castle."

"He told me he comes here frequently to help with the management of the estate."

"Yes, he will probably be paying a visit in a month or two, after the boys return."

"I see," Bella said, and wondered if she could go stay with her grandfather at that time. "You have not . . . received an invitation to his wedding?"

"No. Have you heard from your cousin?"

"No, and I find it very strange that I have not. We have never been separated this long before. On Tuesday it was a month."

"Perhaps you should write to her," Lady de Ros suggested.

"I am not even sure where she is. She was supposed to go with her great-aunt to Warwickshire, but she kept insisting she wouldn't go. I did write to her before I left London and told her I would be at my grandfather's. I had hoped she would at least write to me there," Bella said, sounding very forlorn.

"And you're sure that she and Lord Brooke are definitely affianced? He appeared to be quite enamored of you, when I last saw him."

"He thought I was Isabelle," Bella said. "He thought we were engaged."

"That's a pity. If you had married Lord Brooke, I would have still seen you quite often. And I would have been relieved to see your future so happily settled. I won't live forever, after all. Though of course I will make sure you're provided for when I die."

Bella thought it funny that both her grandparents were anxious to marry her off to "secure her future," and it seemed the most important qualification in their view was whether or not the prospective husband lived nearby. Though she was grateful that they wanted to keep her close. It made such a pleasant change from the sixteen years she'd lived with Lady Strickland, who had made no secret of the fact that she resented Bella's presence.

"You should send a letter to Fenborough Hall and tell your cousin that you're living here now. Perhaps your first letter went astray. And if she's not in residence at Fenborough Hall at the moment, the letter should eventually reach her."

Bella acknowledged the wisdom of this suggestion and immediately went up to her room to compose a letter to Isabelle. While she was gone, Lady de Ros wrote her own letter. To Lord Brooke.

14

Lord Brooke *was* in residence at Bluffton Castle, where he had gone to lick his wounds in solitude. Though as he sat at the breakfast table reflecting on the past few weeks, he came to the conclusion his solitary state had not proven at all helpful. Perhaps it would have been better if he'd embarked on the dissolute career he'd always disdained, numbing his senses with wine and women and reckless spending. But while that might have drowned out the reproachful voices in his head temporarily, he did not think it would have raised him in his own esteem. In fact, he knew it would not. And, as he was feeling lower than he ever had in his life, he didn't think descending into the depths of depravity was quite the prescription he needed.

But the word "prescription" unfortunately brought to mind Bella's doctor-husband, and he was plunged back into a maelstrom of confusion and pain and found himself too depressed to do anything but sit there and stare unseeingly into his coffee. He wished he'd never read the note she'd left, as seeing written in black-and-white how relieved she was that she didn't have to marry him when all he wanted in life was to marry her was a continual torment to him. So when the post was delivered at just that moment he reached for it eagerly, as if it were a rope thrown to a drowning man.

However, it only served to remind him of his distress.

Lady de Ros had written that she was arranging a marriage between her oldest grandson and a newly discovered young relative of hers, who was in residence at Afton Manor and to whom she would be leaving her personal fortune. "I trust you will have no objection to this alliance, as I have been told you are about to embark on an arranged marriage yourself," she wrote.

Lord Brooke looked up from the letter, shocked and dismayed. Allow his beloved sister's son to enter an arranged marriage, with some so-called relative who had popped up from who-knew-where and was most likely a fortune hunter? He would not stand for it! He had always been opposed to arranged marriages, from the time he was a child and he had seen his own sister forced into one. That had been the primary reason he hadn't intended to submit to the alliance that had been arranged for *him*. But when he had met Lady Isabelle again and found himself so enchanted by her, he had fooled himself into thinking that perhaps he had been mistaken in his opposition to such an arrangement. Perhaps, in his case, his parents had chosen just as well as he would have chosen for himself.

But what grief *that* thinking had brought him. He now knew that he would have been far better off had he met Bella without that godforsaken arrangement obscuring matters. One of the many questions that plagued him was whether Bella had eloped with the doctor in part as an act of rebellion against her mother and the arrangement she'd made for her to marry him.

And what did Lady de Ros mean by saying he was about to embark on his own marriage? He supposed since she didn't go about much, she'd had no opportunity to hear what had really occurred. Rumors that Lady Isabelle had eloped with her physician were already spreading. That was the other reason he had buried himself at Bluffton Castle: he could not bear the sympathetic glances he had begun to receive from his friends, and the expressions of glee on the faces of his enemies. It had been obvious to all of London that he had been courting Lady Isabelle before her elopement. And now it was just as obvious that she had jilted him.

He left the breakfast table and went upstairs to pack a small bag. He would pay a visit to Lady de Ros and get to the bottom of this affair. It was his responsibility to protect his poor nephew from the distress his mother, and Lord Brooke himself, had experienced when marriages had been arranged for them. And while doing so he could hopefully forget, for a few moments at least, the woman who had broken his heart.

On the same morning Lord Brooke received a letter from Lady de Ros, Issie received a letter from Bella.

Dr. Jordan, who had been watching her face as she sorted through her correspondence, could tell by her expression that it was from her cousin even before she spoke.

"James!" she said, holding the letter up to show him. "Bella has finally written to me!"

"Don't keep me in suspense. Where is she?"

Issie looked back down at the letter and her brow wrinkled when she saw from whence it came. "She's here in Oxfordshire, though I would have never been able to find her. I've never even *heard* of Afton Manor." There was silence while she read. "She's writing to tell me where she's living and begs me to write to her there. She is serving as a companion to Lady de Ros." There was another pause. "It doesn't appear that she knew I was in residence here, and writes that she hopes her letter finds me." Issie looked pleadingly at James. "Can we go and see her, today?"

"Of course. I'll call the carriage while you change," he said immediately. He knew how devastated Issie had been when they'd returned from their wedding in Gretna Green and Bella was not at Fenborough Hall. Traveling to Scotland and back had taken more than a week, and Issie had been sure Bella would be awaiting her when she returned. And when she was not, Issie had racked her brain trying to figure out where her cousin might have gone, picturing her in all sorts of dire circumstances and blaming herself for leaving London without first speaking with her cousin. A few days ago, Issie had gathered her courage—and now that he'd learned how her mother had mistreated her, he knew how much courage it had required—and had traveled to

Warwickshire to ask her great-aunt if she'd seen or heard from Bella. It was doubtful Lady Dutton would have helped even if she'd had any information to offer, but it had become clear that she did not know any more than they did. The trip was not a total waste, however; they had at least learned that Bella had disappeared from the townhouse on the same morning Isabelle had, which explained why Bella had not joined them at Fenborough Hall. It appeared that Bella had never received Issie's note, as Lady Dutton *had* seen it, and Issie knew that if Bella had found and read it she would never have left it for Lady Dutton to discover.

Surprisingly, Lord Dutton had been very concerned about Bella and had treated Issie far more kindly, asking that she inform him as soon as she discovered Bella's whereabouts and offering to assist in the search.

Issie and James had decided to travel to London and question the staff still in residence at the Duttons' townhouse, but before they could do so they had received Bella's letter.

Therefore, James was more than willing to take a journey that he found, after consulting a map, was only sixteen miles. And he would have traveled much further to appease his wife's anxiety. That was his duty as her doctor *and* her husband.

That afternoon Bella and Lady de Ros were seated in the drawing room when they heard the sound of a carriage in the drive. They looked at each other, and without a word quietly smoothed their skirts and sat up straighter in their seats in a manner that was so strikingly similar that their familial ties would have been evident to anyone who had been present to observe them.

A few minutes later the butler entered, announcing: "Lady Isabelle Jordan and Dr. Jordan," and Issie was suddenly in the doorway. She curtsied to Lady de Ros, but upon catching sight of Bella, she ran to her side and hugged her. Bella, who had risen at the couple's entrance, hugged her back just as tightly, and Lady de Ros and the doctor smiled at each other at the joyous reunion that was unfolding before them.

"Oh, Bella, don't ever do that to me again!" Issie was saying, laughing and crying at the same time. "I was so worried about you! Why did you not go to Fenborough Hall? Or at least write to me weeks ago?"

But Bella, as happy as she was to see her cousin, still had not recovered from her shock when she'd heard the butler announce her name, and wanted that clarified before they discussed anything else. "Issie, I don't understand. Why were you presented as Lady Isabelle *Jordan*? You can't be married to *Dr. Jordan*?"

"Why can't I? What's wrong with that?" Issie asked defensively, and it was obvious by her reaction that she was accustomed to receiving criticism of her marriage. Bella winced inwardly at the thought of how Lady Dutton must have reacted.

"Nothing is wrong with it; if it's true I couldn't be more delighted. But the last time I saw you, you told me you were to marry Lord Brooke."

"What? That's not possible—" Issie paused and thought back to the hectic events of a month earlier. "Oh, I suppose there was a point, right after James rejected me, that I planned to marry Lord Brooke instead—"

"You never told *me* you 'planned' to marry him," Dr. Jordan interjected, and was ignored.

"—but James came to see me the very next morning and apologized and we eloped to Gretna Green. I thought you'd be at Fenborough Hall to meet us upon our return. I assume you didn't receive my note?"

"No. And I suppose you left London before *my* letter was delivered."

"I must have; I've had no correspondence from you. I have been *frantic* with worry."

The inhabitants of the grand salon were so preoccupied with explanations and apologies and rejoicing that they failed to hear another carriage arrive, and their only warning of the next visitor was when the butler announced: "Lord Brooke."

Issie, who had felt a little guilty that she'd broken her unofficial engagement without even a word to the other participant, whirled around to face him as he walked into the room, instinctively grabbing her cousin's hand. Bella was similarly shocked to see him, but her emotions were not so easily defined. As soon as she'd discovered he and Issie were not married, or even engaged, she'd felt such relief that it had made her weak, and when she'd seen him so unexpectedly she'd been grateful Issie was holding on to her because otherwise she might have collapsed. She wondered if he'd been ill; he was paler than usual and he looked fatigued. But he still appeared the most beautiful sight in the world, to her. And when their eyes met she read a similar message in his gaze. However, the expression of joy that had erased the tiredness from his eyes changed a moment later to one of great sadness, even bitterness, and she was suddenly stricken with shame that she'd never told him personally of her deception and apologized for it. She hadn't had a chance to ask Issie if she'd informed him of it, either, so Bella still did not know if he'd been told. It had not yet occurred to her, however, that if he did *not* know that she and Issie had exchanged identities, he would have spent the last month believing *she* was the one married to Dr. Jordan.

Lord Brooke was possibly the most aghast at the sight of Lady de Ros's visitors. He couldn't care less that Miss Grant was there, though he was relieved that no lasting harm had come to her after Lady Dutton had treated her so shabbily. But he had never expected nor wanted to see Bella again now that she was lost to him. Particularly not in the company of her new husband, whom she was so enamored of and who had apparently saved her from the awful fate of marrying him. However, he could not control his reaction when he first saw her, before his mind had caught up with his heart, when their eyes had met and he had fooled himself into thinking he had read in hers the same unspoken message his were sending: "I love you; I am heartbroken without you; you mean everything to me."

There was a long silence as everyone stared at one

another, which was broken at last by Lady de Ros. "Good afternoon, Lord Brooke. How good of you to call."

He turned to look at his hostess in surprise, as he'd forgotten her very existence. But her greeting reminded him that there were meaningless formalities to engage in, and he bowed to her and murmured a response.

He then nodded to Bella and Issie, with a murmured, "Lady Isabelle, Miss Grant." Both ladies bobbed a slight curtsy in response.

Lady de Ros then gestured to her fourth guest. "Lord Brooke, may I present Dr. Jordan to you."

Lord Brooke turned to look at the doctor, and it appeared to those watching as if he was about to refuse the introduction, but he finally gave a slight nod, and said, "Dr. Jordan," to which Dr. Jordan responded with an equally slight nod, perhaps even slighter, and a murmured "Lord Brooke." It was noted by those observing that neither mentioned meeting the other was "a pleasure."

Lady de Ros invited everyone to take a seat and they did so. Lord Brooke, having regained some of his composure, looked over to where Bella and Issie sat side by side and said, "I hear congratulations are in order."

He hadn't intended to be vague, but neither young woman knew to what he was referring. They had just found each other after weeks apart, and so that was at the forefront of their minds, not Issie's marriage. Besides, he seemed to be looking at Bella, not Issie, though it was difficult to tell, as they were seated so close to each other. But Dr. Jordan, who was feeling slightly affronted at the arrogant manner in which Lord Brooke had reacted when introduced to him, and whose masculine vanity was suffering anyway at the newfound knowledge that this good-looking son-of-an . . . earl had been his rival for Issie's affections, took it upon himself to respond. "Thank you, Lord Brooke," he said. "Lady Isabelle and I are very happy."

Lord Brooke, who had turned to look at the doctor when he spoke, immediately turned back toward Bella with such a burning look of reproach and despair, that she instantly realized he had not been informed of who she really was, and was suffering under the misapprehension that she was married to someone else. She couldn't bear to let him continue to believe this, as she had until recently held the same mistaken belief about *him*, and the distress it had caused her had been nearly unbearable.

But just as Bella opened her mouth to speak, she heard Issie say: "I *am* sorry, Lord Brooke, for not formally releasing you from our engagement, but it did not seem to me that you wanted to marry me anyway. You looked at me that first time we met as if I were a bug you'd prefer to squash."

Lord Brooke's anguished expression changed to one of confusion. "I beg your pardon," he said, and it was obvious he thought Issie had lost her mind.

Bella put a restraining hand on Issie's arm. "He doesn't know who we really are," she said. "Unless you told him?"

"No, I never did. But didn't you?" Issie asked.

"I did not have the opportunity, either."

Lord Brooke interrupted them to say: "If one of you

would tell me now, I'd be delighted to know what you're talking about."

Bella turned to look at him. "I am more sorry than I can say to have deceived you this way, but I am actually Arabella Grant, Lady Isabelle's cousin. This young lady is the *true* Lady Isabelle," Bella said, nodding at Issie. "My cousin is in poor health—we did not deceive you about that—so she did not feel like she could participate in her London season and begged me to take her place. I had no idea the two of you were engaged or I would have never agreed to do so." Bella gave Issie a sideways glance that caused Issie to turn red and lower her head in embarrassment. It was obvious that, while Bella was not one to hold a grudge and very quick to extend forgiveness, this omission on Issie's part would take her a little longer to forget.

"Then *she* is married to Dr. Jordan?" Lord Brooke asked, and though he had been taught it was impolite to point, he felt in this case he could be forgiven this solecism and gestured to Issie. And then, to verify what he felt was the most important piece of information that had been disclosed, he asked Bella, "And *you* are unmarried?"

"As of this moment," Bella said, and though her eyes were watery, her irrepressible grin had peeked out.

Lord Brooke closed his eyes briefly and murmured, "Thank God," and Bella felt like saying "Amen" to his brief prayer but restrained herself. He then opened his eyes and, jumping up from his seat, went over to Dr. Jordan and offered him his hand. "May I offer you the sincerest of congratulations," he said warmly, shaking Dr. Jordan's hand vigorously, to that man's amazement.

He then turned to Issie. "Lady Isabelle, it is I who must apologize to you. I never thought of you as a, what is it you said, a bug I wanted to squash? I was horrified at the thought of an arranged marriage and would have appeared discontented when presented to any young woman. I was also displeased by your mother's unkind treatment of you, and your obvious unhappiness. But I can see that you've matured into an attractive, sensible young lady, and I truly am delighted that you've made a match based on love and mutual esteem, instead of that cold-blooded union our parents had arranged for us. May I kiss the bride?" he asked, waiting first for Issie's nod and then looking toward the doctor as well before kissing Issie briefly but enthusiastically on the cheek. Issie was blushing a little, and Bella was, too, as she couldn't help comparing that cousinly kiss with other, far more passionate kisses Lord Brooke had bestowed on a different "Lady Isabelle."

"And now, with your permission, Lady de Ros, I would like to hear a longer explanation—and apology—from the erstwhile Lady Belle, in private," Lord Brooke said, looking at Bella in a way that conveyed that she had not been unconditionally forgiven and he still intended to exact punishment. But as Bella was not the least bit afraid of Lord Brooke, who she knew was incapable of behaving cruelly to her, the thought of whatever penance he might exact didn't alarm her at all, and instead caused her to feel a tingle of anticipation.

"I am not sure if I *should* give my permission," Lady de Ros said, to the couple's dismay, and they both turned to look at her, Bella saying, "But . . . Rossie . . ."

"I assume you're here in response to my letter, Lord Brooke," Lady de Ros continued, ignoring Bella's protest, and Lord Brooke nodded in confirmation of her statement. "Then I should tell you that I recently discovered Arabella is a relative of mine, and I intend to arrange for her to marry my grandson so that she can officially return to the family and live at Afton Manor permanently. I also intend to leave my personal fortune to her upon my death."

Bella, who knew nothing of the letter that Lady de Ros had written to Lord Brooke, or of her plans for her, was stunned. However, she had no intention of agreeing to them. Before she could say so, Lord Brooke intervened.

"Lady de Ros, as your grandson's guardian, I unequivo-cally refuse to give my consent to such a match. Because, though I am adamantly opposed to arranged marriages, I am determined to make an exception and arrange a marriage for myself." He then turned to look at Bella. "With Miss Grant."

Bella put out her hand to Lord Brooke, and he grasped it and raised it to his lips. Issie, who had only just realized that Bella and Lord Brooke were in love, was a little put out by his stated intention to marry Bella. Even though Issie loved her husband and knew he loved her, she still was slightly possessive of the cousin who had been the only one to love her for so long, and she had had a different plan in mind. "But . . . she was to live with me and Dr. Jordan at Fenborough Hall," she said.

"I am sorry, young lady, but she was to live here with me," Lady de Ros contradicted her.

"I believe Bella should be the one to decide where she will live, and I'd like to put another option before her," Lord Brooke said, still retaining his beloved's hand and pulling her in the direction of the door.

Bella was more than willing to go with him, but looked back over her shoulder to say, "Excuse me for a moment," before disappearing through the doorway, as she did feel it was rather rude to leave her cousin alone with her grandmother. Lady de Ros was just the type of haughty older woman who unnerved Issie so. (At least that's how her grandmother appeared, though Bella knew that she wasn't really like that.) But Dr. Jordan would watch over Issie now, Bella reminded herself, and felt a pang very similar to the one Issie had felt earlier. It was difficult for Bella to relinquish her role as Issie's protector, even though she had always assumed she'd happily do so. Some habits were hard to break, and it had been her responsibility to love and protect her younger cousin her entire life. Even when that had led her into her present predicament.

Her present predicament, being very familiar with his nephew's estate, had guided her into the library. He opened his mouth to speak, but then silently and abruptly pulled her into his arms and held her tightly against him. She hugged him back just as hard, and after a few moments spent holding each other as if daring anybody or anything to try to separate them, he finally said, echoing Issie's comment, though he did not know it, "Don't ever do that to me again."

"What exactly am I not supposed to do, my lord?" Bella asked. Lord Brooke pulled away from her and led her to a backless chaise in front of the window, where they both sat facing each other, Lord Brooke still holding one of Bella's hands and gently caressing it.

"You are never to leave me again. Not for one day. Not for one hour," he said possessively, and though some might rebel at such a statement, Bella was thrilled by it.

"I would gladly promise such a thing if it were possible, but I can see that there might be circumstances where it would prove impractical."

"How dare you talk to me of practicalities at a time like this," he said, before kissing her. And his kisses were so convincing that Bella was ready to promise that she wouldn't leave his side for one *minute,* if she had been given the opportunity to speak. Though after a few moments in his embrace, she realized that speech was overrated, and that feelings could be communicated just as well, if not better, by touch, and so she concentrated her efforts on convincing him how much she loved him by running her hands through his hair, lightly caressing his neck, and measuring the breadth and strength of his shoulders. It appeared he had a similar goal in mind, as his hands were slowly tracing the contours of her back and waist, as if he were a potter and he was molding them together. However, contrary to the command he'd just given her never to leave his side, he pulled back suddenly, jumping up from the chaise and walking away from her.

He was breathing very rapidly and it took him a moment to catch his breath so that he could speak. "Bella, we must be married immediately," he said.

This seemed entirely reasonable to Bella, who nodded her agreement, as she was also out of breath and didn't know if she *could* speak.

"But first, please explain to me why you pretended to be your cousin, why you did not confide in me even after it was obvious I'd come to care for you, and then compounded everything by allowing me to believe you'd married someone else!"

And Bella, stabbed to the heart by the pain she heard in his voice, got up from her seat to run over and throw herself into his arms, holding him tightly in an attempt at consolation. "I am so very, *very* sorry; I never meant to hurt you. I know exactly how you feel, as I thought you were married to Issie."

"What?" Lord Brooke asked, before breaking away from her, and backing up even further when she instinctively followed him. "No, please stay away from me, Bella, while you explain. I can't concentrate when you're so close," he said, his gaze darting over her face and figure so longingly she began to tremble and saw the wisdom in what he was saying. She returned to the chaise while he threw himself into a chair opposite, and then she proceeded to explain in more detail the reason for her masquerade, telling him of how ill Issie had been when they'd first arrived in London and how she'd begged Bella to take her place, and how Bella had reluctantly agreed.

"I never expected to fall in love with you during what was supposed to be my one season masquerading as Lady Belle, but, after I did, I wanted to tell you who I really was. However, Issie persuaded me to wait until the season was over, so that Lady Dutton would not have to know we'd deceived her. And if you knew how badly Issie has been treated, first by her mother and then her great-aunt, you'd understand why I wanted to protect her from Lady Dutton's wrath," Bella said, and she saw from Lord Brooke's expression he did understand, to some degree, and sympathized. "In Issie's defense, I never told her of my feelings for you, or I'm sure she would have told me about your arranged marriage. And that last night, in the gardens, I was going to tell you the truth, but that is when you told me you were engaged to Lady Isabelle. And I thought you'd merely paid court to me because you thought I was her."

"What? How could you have thought *that*? If I hadn't become enamored of you almost from the first moment we met I would have never pursued you. I had no intention of fulfilling our mothers' plans for me and Lady Isabelle to marry and, since our engagement was never official, I had decided to convey my lack of intentions by not paying her any attention at all. If I hadn't run into you in the halls of St. James's Palace, and quite literally been bowled over by you, I would never have even called on 'Lady Isabelle' during her season. I have quite an aversion to arranged marriages, you know. My sister was forced into one, and was very unhappy as a result.

"And I was very right to think Lady Isabelle and I would not have suited," Lord Brooke said, shaking his head and smiling at the thought of just how unsuited they were to each other. "I know you adore her, Bella, but I'm very grateful that she's now Dr. Jordan's responsibility and not yours. Hopefully, he will not give in to her every whim, as you apparently do."

"I do not give in to her *every* whim. But I could not help indulging her a little. She was so very deprived for so long, you can have no idea," Bella said.

"I think I have some idea, and I'm glad she had you to look after her," Lord Brooke said, with a warm smile. Bella's loyalty toward her cousin was one of the reasons he loved her so very much. He could only be grateful she was so generous with her affection, and that she was also willing to bestow it upon him. But Bella startled him when she became very serious all of a sudden and said: "I am not sure I will suit you any better than Issie, Lord Brooke."

"What foolishness is this? I seem to recall you saying you loved me, and you can be in no doubt now of my love for you."

"Of course I love you, quite desperately, so much so that I had thought any prospect of happiness was over when I was forced to give you up. But, unlike Issie, I was never trained to be the wife of an earl. I have none of the qualifications your bride should have," she confessed. "You should look higher for a wife, my lord."

Lord Brooke stood and crossed back over to Bella's side. "What are these so-called qualifications? I could never find a woman more suited to me than you, Bella. Should I tell you what *my* qualifications are? I require a wife who is compassionate and forgiving and intelligent, and if she happens to have the most luscious figure ever possessed by a mortal woman, well, that's an unexpected and much-appreciated bonus," Lord Brooke said, whispering that last qualification into Bella's ear, before dropping a kiss on her neck. And then he spent a few more minutes demonstrating to Bella, without the use of words, just how very well they were suited to each other.

But there were still explanations and plans to be made, and eventually they returned to their earlier conversation. "I'm glad you ended up here after you left Lady Dutton's. I was very concerned about you, even when I didn't know 'Miss Grant' was actually the woman I loved. Though I have no idea *how* you ended up with Lady de Ros. Are you really related to her?"

Bella nodded. "You mustn't tell anyone, but she is my grandmother."

Lord Brooke shook his head in disbelief. "You are going to have to explain all of this to me again, very slowly, after we are married. I used to think myself quick-witted, but that was before I met you and your cousin and became involved in your convoluted schemes."

He stood up, drawing Bella with him. "You did agree to marry me immediately, correct? That was not a passion-induced fantasy of mine?"

"Since you are quite sure that *you* want to marry *me*, I will marry you as quickly as it can be arranged. I suffered terribly, too, this past month. I have no desire to be separated from you a moment more than I have to."

Lord Brooke's heart was so full he thought it might burst at this declaration from the woman he loved. He contented himself with kissing both of her hands in acknowledgment and farewell, as he knew if he took her in his arms again it would be quite awhile before he could bring himself to leave. "Then I will go to London immediately and procure a special license. I'll be back in two days and we can marry the day after."

Bella had no objection to this plan, though one problem had occurred to her. "But what are we to tell people, after we are married, when they recognize me as Lady Belle?"

"The truth: that you're Lady Isabelle's cousin, and you are so alike that even Lady Isabelle's great-aunt had difficulty telling you apart."

15

Issie and Lady de Ros, seeing how happy Bella was, quickly overcame any disappointment they might have initially felt over sharing their beloved Bella with Lord Brooke, who couldn't ever even *hope* to be worthy of her, and began planning how soon after her wedding Bella could come to visit them. Though they nearly got into another argument over that. Bella finally reminded them that they both could come visit her at Bluffton Castle anytime they wanted for as long as they wanted, even at the same time, and was able to smooth things over.

Lady de Ros tried to talk Bella into waiting at least a few weeks longer, but Bella was adamant that she was marrying Lord Brooke the day after he returned from London with the special license. So Lady de Ros graciously gave in, and invited Issie and her husband to stay until the wedding, an invitation they accepted, sending a groom back to

Fenborough Hall to collect their things. Lady de Ros also sent a wedding invitation to Mr. Perry, and sent for a seamstress to come and make her granddaughter the most beautiful wedding gown the world had ever seen.

The evening before Bella's wedding, Lady de Ros went to her room, followed by a maidservant holding a heavy case.

"Put it there, Maggie," Lady de Ros instructed the maidservant, and she obediently placed it on the table Lady de Ros had indicated before leaving. "I wanted you to have a necklace of mine to wear on your wedding day. Pick out whatever you would like."

Bella, who had been gazing out of the window with a dreamy expression on her face, turned to her grandmother. "That is so kind of you, Rossie, and I'm sure all of your jewelry is beautiful, but I'd like to wear the necklace my mother wore on *her* wedding day," Bella said. She then went and pulled her mother's necklace out of a drawer and showed it to her grandmother.

Lady de Ros looked shocked by the sight of it, and Bella grew a little defensive, thinking her grandmother thought it too paltry a thing to wear to wed an earl. "I believe the pearls are real, though the diamond *is* paste," Bella said.

"It is not paste," Lady de Ros said, and her eyes were suspiciously damp. "I gave this to Mr. Perry for your mother when he took her to live with him and his wife. It's a real diamond. I thought if she ever needed money she could sell it. And it made me happy that I could provide for her in some manner. And that her father could as well, unbeknownst to him. He gave it to me," Lady de Ros said, and her cheeks turned red and she lowered her eyes.

"I see," Bella said, and she remembered Lord Dutton's expression when he'd seen this same necklace, and realized she now knew who her *real* grandfather was.

She said nothing to Lady de Ros about that, however, as she felt that if her grandmother had wanted her to know who her grandfather was, she would have told her. Instead, Bella embraced her very tenderly, and wished that it had been possible for Rossie to have married the man *she'd* loved, as Bella was about to do.

Lord Brooke had invited two other guests to the wedding while he was in London, and the morning after he returned with the special license, Catherine Adams arrived at Afton Manor on the arm of Mr. Peckham. When Bella heard she was there, she sent a maid to bring Catherine to her chamber, as Bella had washed her hair and was waiting for it to dry and couldn't go down to greet her.

Bella was overjoyed to see Catherine, who was just as happy to see her and clasped Bella a little too forcefully to her chest, as she was prone to do. Bella was eventually released, gasping for breath, as Catherine informed her that Lord Brooke had explained everything, and that Catherine was also engaged, to Mr. Charles Peckham.

"When I explained to Charles that his behavior toward you was not that of a gentleman, he was so very mortified and begged me to help him improve. Well, it was the first time someone thought that *I* was qualified to instruct *them* on proper behavior," she said with a shocked look. "And Charles's uncle is a duke! So I told him about my family, and that I wasn't really related to the Hampshire Adamses, and he did not care one whit! I hope you are not upset, Lady Belle. I mean, Miss Grant—"

"Please, call me Bella. And why would I be upset?"

"Well, I know Charles had initially been one of your beaux, and you might think that I had stolen him from you."

"Not at all! I think you and Mr. Peckham are ideally suited. You're both so kind and friendly and such cheerful company," Bella said, and didn't once think that Catherine was ridiculous to believe Bella was pining for Mr. Peckham when she was marrying the incomparable Lord Brooke. Bella considered it a very obvious case of love being blind, as it was apparent that Catherine was head over heels for the man she'd previously despised.

Catherine stayed to help Bella get dressed, to the disapproval of Issie, who could not totally overcome the feeling that Bella had belonged to *her* before all of these other people, and that she should at least be able to have her to herself this last time. Bella, sensing Issie's feelings, asked Catherine if she would leave them alone together. Catherine cheerfully agreed and went down to the drawing room.

"Issie, you know that I've loved you since you were two and I will love you forever," Bella said.

"I know. And now you've chosen to love that man, as well, even though he's not at all worthy of you. Your taste is consistently terrible," Issie said, with a sniff.

"Do not insult the people I love," Bella told her. "Or my taste. It is impeccable."

"Oh, Bella," Issie said, crying in earnest. "I will miss you so very much."

"You will not miss me as much as you expect. You have James now, and soon you will have little Jameses, and little Issies, and you will barely even think of me, except to wonder why I come to visit so often."

"I will never forget you, Bella," Issie vowed.

"Then how could you think I'd ever forget you?" Bella asked. "And now you've made me look ugly for my own wedding," she complained, putting her fingers to her eyes in a useless attempt to catch the tears before they fell.

"That's impossible. You could never be ugly," Issie said, but she helped Bella apply a damp handkerchief to her face, and they both managed to stop crying and reapply themselves to the serious business of making themselves look beautiful.

"And Issie, you do know, I hope, that Lord Brooke never intended to make you feel bad about yourself. He never was repulsed by you or thought that you were ugly, even if you did think he felt that way. I would hate it if the two people I loved most didn't like each other."

"Don't worry; I feel much better about myself now. James thinks I'm the most beautiful woman in the world, and the brightest person he's ever known, male or female. And I feel like it's true, when I'm around him," Issie said, blushing.

"I knew the first time he laid his head on your breast that you were destined to be together."

"He's a *doctor*, Bella!" Issie said admonishingly, before breaking into giggles. And when Grandpa Perry arrived to escort the bride down the stairs, he found her and her cousin lying on the bed, laughing like little children.

The vows were exchanged, the wedding cake eaten, and Bella was hugged and kissed more that day than she'd been the first twenty years of her life.

But finally the time came that Lord Brooke had been eagerly anticipating: they said goodbye to their friends and family and left in a carriage bound for Bluffton Castle, where they were to spend their honeymoon.

"I was so jealous of Issie, when I was fifteen, that she was able to visit a castle and I wasn't allowed to go with her," Bella said, after she'd finished waving goodbye and had settled back in her seat.

"Imagine if you *had* accompanied them; the past few months would have never happened."

"Because I would not have been able to masquerade as Issie, you mean, since you would have met us both when we were younger and recognized me right away?"

"Perhaps, but I think it more likely that I would have fallen in love with you the first time we met and insisted on courting you as soon as you were old enough. You'd be living with me at Bluffton Castle right now."

"I'm not sure you would have fallen in love with me at fifteen," Bella said. "I had spots."

Lord Brooke used this as an excuse to run a finger over his bride's flawless, smooth skin, before saying: "I am absolutely certain I would have fallen in love with you, even with spots."

When he bent to kiss her, Bella pulled back even though she was very eager to receive more of his kisses—the ones she'd received that morning from friends and family paled in comparison to those of her new husband. However, she had a serious matter to discuss with him first.

"Wait. I don't know what to call you. You never told me your name."

Lord Brooke blinked, and then began laughing. "*I* never told you *my* name? That's quite the accusation, considering that when we met, you were the one masquerading under a false name."

"Yes, but I told you my real name almost from the first. I told you I was called Bella."

"And I told you what to call me," Lord Brooke said.

"You did?" Bella asked.

"You are to call me *my* lord Brooke and I am to call you *my* lady Bella," he said, his voice low and husky. Bella was prepared to accept that answer, as she figured they'd talked long enough, and the way he'd just pronounced her name and called her "his" had made her shiver. Still, she did think she should know and use her husband's name, so she persisted. "But you never told me your Christian name. The first I heard of it was during the wedding service. It is William, is it not?"

"It is. Why does that make you grin?"

"Because that's Shakespeare's name. And Issie *idolizes* William Shakespeare."

"'What's in a name? That which we call a rose by any other name would smell as sweet,'" he murmured, and Bella thought it was a very good thing he had never quoted Shakespeare to Issie, or she would have been unable to resist him. And then William was kissing her, and soon she couldn't think at all.

Six Months Later

Bella was practicing the piano. Not because she particularly wanted to, but because in her new role as the wife of an earl she figured she should acquire *some* ladylike accomplishments. Also, William had gone to town and she missed him desperately and was trying to distract herself. However, she found that playing the piano was not at all effective in redirecting her thoughts away from her husband, and she sunk into a sad reverie, absentmindedly plunking a key here and there.

"I would hardly call that 'professhent,'" William said. He had entered the room, unbeknownst to Bella, and was observing his wife's lackluster performance with a loving smile.

Bella, turning and seeing him standing just a few feet away, gave a little screech and jumped up from the bench to throw herself into arms that were already reaching for her.

"You're back earlier than I expected," Bella said, when she could speak.

"I couldn't stay away a moment longer. I sacrificed a night's sleep to get here a day early and should probably retire to bed immediately. Would Lady Brooke care to join me?" he asked, dropping very persuasive kisses on her neck.

"To sleep?" Bella asked.

"We could do that, too."

After William had bathed, eaten, and taken care of other, more important matters, he remembered he had something he hadn't yet told Bella.

"Oh, I have a bit of bad news for you, I'm afraid," he said, pulling a little away from his wife, who had been lying drowsily in his arms in bed even though it was midafternoon. However, she was contemplating staying there the rest of the day, and letting the servants think what they chose.

Hearing the serious note in William's voice, she became fully alert and sat up. "What is it?"

"Lord Dutton passed away last week. I was contacted by his attorney while I was in town. It appears he left our future daughter something in his will."

Bella had told William that she suspected Lord Dutton was her grandfather, so neither of them was as surprised at the bequest as they otherwise would have been, as it appeared to confirm Bella's theory. "Our future . . . *daughter*?" she asked, after her initial shock and sadness at the news of

Lord Dutton's death had dissipated a little and she was able to focus on the second part of the announcement.

"Yes. He left her a small fortune: a dowry of twenty thousand pounds. But only on the condition we do not arrange a marriage for her. She is to be allowed to choose her own husband," Lord Brooke said.

Bella wondered if this stipulation was because Lord Dutton had not been able to choose his own bride, or if it was because he had witnessed Issie and Lord Brooke narrowly avoid a disastrous match.

"And if she is as wise as her mother, as I fully anticipate she will be, I have no doubt she will make the best possible choice. As you did," Lord Brooke said, running his hand through his wife's tousled hair and grinning mischievously at her.

"So *you* were the best choice I could have made?" Bella said, reaching for her husband before whispering in his ear: "Prove it."

Author's Note

I hope you had as much fun reading this book as I had writing it! However, it's not all fun and games working on a historical romantic comedy; I also do a lot of *very* serious research. While writing this one I learned about the correct attire for a court presentation, art exhibitions at the Royal Academy, and lectures at the Surrey Institution. I also delved into bridges and the invention of stethoscopes. Here are a few things of note regarding these last two items:

Those of you who have seen London's Waterloo Bridge or plan to visit it, please keep in mind that the current bridge is not the same as the one described in the pages of this book. The first Waterloo Bridge opened in 1817 but was later demolished and replaced by the current one, which opened in 1942. You can still see "the noblest bridge in the world," however, through the work of numerous artists including Claude Monet, who painted it at least forty times from his window at the Savoy Hotel.

And if you're curious why Dr. Jordan didn't use a stethoscope to listen to Issie's heart, that instrument hadn't yet been introduced in 1818, though French doctor René Laënnec began developing one around that time. Dr. Laënnec had been hesitant to apply his ear to a young lady's chest during an examination and wrote in a treatise published in 1819: "I rolled sheets of paper into a kind of cylinder and applied one end of it to the region of the heart and the other to my ear, and was not a little surprised and pleased to find that I could thereby perceive the action of the heart in a manner much more clear and distinct than I had ever been able to do by the immediate application of the ear." His findings were translated into English in 1821, and it is to be supposed that Dr. Jordan began using a stethoscope himself at that point, and thereby protected his female patients from experiencing nervous palpitations brought on, not by an underlying heart condition, but by the attractive doctor's disturbing proximity.

Acknowledgments

Thank you, first and foremost, to readers of this book, and especially those of you who laughed while reading!

Many thanks to my editor, Kate Seaver, for her kind collaboration, invaluable help, and insightful comments. I also appreciate the hard work of Amanda Maurer, Danielle Keir, Stephanie Felty, and Hannah Engler at Berkley, as well as those who help to produce my beautiful book covers. And a huge thank-you to my wonderful, kind, and brilliant agent, Stefanie Lieberman, and the rest of the team at Janklow & Nesbit, especially Molly Steinblatt and Adam Hobbins.

I'd also like to warmly thank Serena Moyle, library curator at Hearth & Soul, who has hosted so many amazing events to celebrate my books and has been an absolute dream to work with. I'm grateful as well to the staff at Midtown Reader in Tallahassee, Florida, who arrange to get signed copies to readers locally and nationally and have also been fabulous hosts. I'd also like to send a grateful shout-out to Happy Medium Books Café in Jacksonville, Florida, and The Bookshelf in Thomasville, Georgia. And a special thanks to those who have attended my book events at these and other venues; your support means so much to me! I appreciate, too, the Bookstagrammers, bloggers, podcast hosts, fellow authors, and all who have helped spread the word about my work by posting lovely reviews and/or pictures.

To Ceci Sproule, for being an early reader of this book: Thank you so much! And to the rest of my NY friends, especially Justin Price and Ryan Serrano: y'all are awesome and I appreciate your support personally and professionally. To my sisters, Charlotte and Vicky, who make time to read early copies of *all* of my books: I love you both! Sorry I'm the baby of the family and such a drama queen. Finally, to Jonathan, the most supportive husband in the world: thanks for loving me, marrying me, and giving me my own happily-ever-after.

Photo by Jonathan Allain

Suzanne Allain is a screenwriter and the author of *Mr. Malcolm's List*, *Miss Lattimore's Letter*, and *The Ladies Rewrite the Rules*. She lived in New York and Beijing before returning to her hometown of Tallahassee, Florida, where she lives with her husband.

VISIT SUZANNE ALLAIN ONLINE

SuzanneAllain.com

Ready to find
your next great read?

Let us help.

Visit prh.com/nextread

Penguin
Random
House